The Old Room

by

Carl Ewald

Double9 BOOKS

The Old Room

by Carl Ewald

ISBN: 978-93-71463-54-6

Published by

DOUBLE 9 BOOKS
2/13-B, Ansari Road
Daryaganj, New Delhi – 110002
info@double9books.com
www.double9books.com
Tel. 011-40042856

ABOUT THE AUTHOR

Carl Ewald was a Danish novelist, essayist, and satirist best remembered for his literary fairy tales and subtle social commentary. Born on October 15, 1856, in the Duchy of Schleswig, he was the son of Herman Frederik Ewald, a clergyman and writer. His early life was shaped by Denmark's political tensions and cultural shifts, which later influenced his satirical tone. Educated in Copenhagen, he initially pursued a career in forestry before turning to literature full time. His prose is characterized by clarity, irony, and a blend of whimsy with pointed critique, often using allegory to reflect on societal hypocrisy and human frailty. Ewald's fairy tales were not solely for children; they carried layers of meaning that appealed to adult readers and explored questions of morality, tradition, and individuality. His private life was complex—he had two sons, Jesper Ewald and Poul Henningsen, the latter becoming a renowned architect and critic. Though Ewald died relatively young at 51 in Charlottenlund on February 23, 1908, his influence endured through his descendants and his sharp yet elegant body of work, which remains part of Danish literary heritage.

CONTENTS

PART I
CORDT

CHAPTER I

THE room looks out upon the square, which is so big and so fashionable that there is no business done in it.

By day there is a sound of carriages, but at a distance; for the house that contains the room is thrust a long way back and its walls are as thick as the walls of a castle. In the evening, the square shines with a thousand lights; at night, you can hear the rippling of the fountain, which never begins and never stops, cries, no one knowing what they are, and solitary steps that approach and retreat again.

The room is built high over the square. Its window is a door and leads to a balcony filled with red flowers. When the wind lashes them, their petals fly right over into the basin of the fountain and rock upon the water.

The room is long and deep.

Where the window is, the light streams in through the wide, stained-glass panes; but, inside, where the fireplace rises to the ceiling, it is always dark.

No one has ever seen the curtain drawn before the window. But, even if the sun could shine right into the room, it would never have seen a human being there. By day, the room is dead.

It is placed so strangely in the house that it seems to form no part of it. The life of every day passes outside it; and, even when the whole house is lighted up and the horses paw the ground in the gateway and glasses clink and music sounds in the great drawing-room, the door of the room remains constantly closed.

No one has ever crossed its threshold but the master of the house and his wife and the oldest servant in their employ.

For the room is the soul of the house and its tradition and its secret chamber.

It was destined for this purpose long ago by the man who built the house; and so cunningly did he contrive it that no one could guess that it was there, unless he knew of it. Then, when the work was ended, he sealed the architect's tongue with a solemn oath and a heavy fee and the man kept his sworn word.

And the builder of the house decorated the room as richly as was possible according to the means of those days, with gilt and figured leather hangings and stained-glass window-panes and costly carpets from the East. But he placed no furniture in it until the very last. Then he brought two splendid armchairs which he had had made for him in Milan.

They were odd-looking chairs. They glided so smoothly over the floor that a child could move them, and were so large that people became quite small when they sat in them. Their woodwork was carved into birds and animals, whose faces grinned strangely in the dark but ceased to do so when the lights were lit.

When everything was thus ordered for the best, he called an old servant, who had been in the house since he was a child, gave him a key of the room and told him to care for it faithfully. Every evening, when it grew dusk, he was to light the candles on the mantelpiece and he was to do this even if he knew that his master was travelling in distant lands. Every morning, he was to adjust the room with his own hands. None but himself was ever to cross the threshold.

On the evening of the day when he took possession of his house, the master, having first shown her all its other beauties, brought his wife to the room.

She looked round in wonder. But he made her sit in one of the great chairs, seated himself in the other and spoke to her in these words:

"Sweetheart, this room is for you and me and for none other in the world. I have placed it in the most secluded part of the house, far from the counting-house, where we work, from the passages, along which our servants go, and from the drawing-room, where we receive our guests, ay, even from our marriage-bed, where you will sleep by my side."

She took his hand and kissed it and looked at him.

"It shall be the temple of our marriage, hallowed by our love, which is greater than anything that we know. Here we will pray to Him Who gave us to each other. Here we will talk gladly and earnestly every evening when our hearts impel us to. And, when we come to die, our son shall bring his wife here and they shall do as we did."

Thereupon he wrote down in a document how all this had happened and they both sealed it with their names. He hid the document in a secret recess in the wall. And, when all this was accomplished, they fell upon their knees and, folding their hands together, offered a simple prayer to God before they went to rest.

These two are long since dead. But their son complied with their will and his son after him and so on and so forth until the present day.

And, however riches might increase or diminish with the varying fortunes of the times, the old house in the square continued in the possession of the family. For he who was its head always lived in such a way that he kept his ancestral home.

The room stood untouched, as was appointed, and the document grew old and yellow in the secret recess in the wall. Once only in the time of each master of the house was it taken out; and that was on the evening when he first brought his young wife to the secret chamber. Then they wrote their names upon it and put it away again.

But it became the custom for each of them that took lawful possession of the room to adorn it with a piece of furniture after his own taste and heart. And they were strange objects that, in the course of time, gathered round the two great, strange chairs.

There was one of the owners of the house who was kindly and cheerful to the end. He placed in the room, in his wife's honor, a costly spinning-wheel, richly inlaid, which whirred merrily every evening for many a good year and which stood as it was, with thread upon the spindle.

There was one whose thoughts were always roaming and never at rest and whose intellect was obscured before he died. He presented the room with an ingenious representation of the heavenly system. When a spring was pressed, the spheres lit up and ran their eternal courses; and he sat and played with the stars to his last day.

There was another whose wife dreaded the deep silence of the room and never entered it but once. He waited for five years and then had a doll made, a woman, life-size and beautifully dressed. He put it on a chair in the window, so that the light fell on its vacant face. But his son, who loved his mother, drew the doll back, so that it was hidden in the curtain.

There was one whose wife was in the habit of singing when she was sad, as she often was. She brought a spinet, with slender, beautiful notes, which sang like a mother singing her child to sleep. In time, its sound grew very thin. When it was played upon in the room at night, it sounded over the silent square like a humming in the air; and none that passed knew what it was.

There was also one who had his wife's portrait painted and hung the picture on the wall. He broke his wedding-vows and his grandson took the picture down. But, where it had been, a light stain remained that could not be removed.

The man who was master of the house at the time when that happened which is related in this book had brought nothing as yet. But his wife had set up a thing that had caught her eye more than all that she had seen in the way of art on her long travels. This was a jar of a preposterous shape, large and bright and of a pale tint. On one side was the figure of a naked man writhing through thorns. It stood on a stone pedestal hewn from a rock near Jerusalem.

That was how the room was.

Each evening, when it grew dark, the oldest servant in the house lit the candles on the mantelpiece. Each morning, before any one was awake, he cleaned the room with his own hands and watered the red flowers on the balcony. When winter came, he strewed bread-crumbs for the sparrows that gathered on the baluster and twittered.

But the name of him that owned the house was Cordt. And his wife was Fru Adelheid.

CHAPTER II

Cordt sat in one of the armchairs by the chimney, reading.

He was in evening clothes and held his crush-hat and his gloves on his knees. He turned the pages quickly. Every moment, he swept his thick hair from his forehead; every moment, he looked at Fru Adelheid, who was walking up and down the floor with her hands behind her back.

She was very tall and slender. Her face was as white as her white gown. Her mouth was very red, her eyes looked large and strange. She wore flowers in her hair and at her waist.

"You are not reading, Cordt," she said; but she passed with her back to him.

He closed the book and laid it aside. Then he moved the chair so as to turn his face towards her. His eyes were larger than hers and steadier, his mouth firmer.

"How beautiful you are!" he said.

She laughed softly and took his hand and kissed it:

"How charming of you!" she said.

She began to walk again. He stretched out his legs and lay with his head back in the chair, but followed her all the time with his eyes. Now and again, she stopped, smoothed her gown, let her fingers stray over the keys of the spinet and then went out on the balcony through the open door. He could not see her from where he was sitting, but the white train of her dress lay inside the room and he looked at that.

Then she returned, sat on the arm of the other chair and swung her foot to and fro.

"I do not like you to be in good spirits, Adelheid," he said.

Her eyes shone. She looked at the fireplace, where a log lay glowing:

"You should drink a glass of wine, Cordt."

"I do not care for wine."

"No more do I. But I like its exhilaration. It makes one so light-hearted. Then everything becomes so charming."

"Have you been drinking?"

"But, Cordt ... what makes you ask that?"

"Because you are so light-hearted and I so charming."

She went up to him and laid her cheek against his hair:

"Now don't spoil it for me," she said. "You can, with a single word, and that would be a great, great sin. You say I am pretty; and I am glad because you think so and because I am going out with you and because you are handsome and belong to me. We shall be far from each other and close together for all that. We shall nod to each other, as we always do, and know what we know."

He released himself from her gently:

"Sit down a little," he said, "and talk to me."

She kissed him and sat down in the chair and then and there forgot her despondency. Her eyes shone as before. He raked out the embers and threw a log upon them. They sat and watched it catch fire and saw the smoke surround it and rise up. Her foot tapped the carpet; he shaded his eyes with his hand and pursued his thoughts:

"In my first year at the university," he said, "there were five of us who were chums and we used to meet every Saturday evening. It was generally at my rooms, for I could best afford it. We used to sit and drink wine until bright daylight and then take one another home."

"You must have drunk a great deal."

"I don't know. Perhaps we did. We talked so loud and deep. The wine made us feel bigger, braver and cleverer. Next day, we were quite different, more reserved and cool. But we could look one another boldly in the face, for we had nothing to repent of. It did not matter if we had allowed ourselves to be carried away. We knew one another so well and trusted one another."

She sat and looked at him as he spoke, but said nothing. Lost in thought, he continued to throw logs on the fire until she took one out of his hand and put it aside:

"You'll set the house on fire!"

"One should never drink wine with strangers," he said. "You see, it is so degrading to be stripped bare. And that is just what happens."

"You say that as if it meant getting drunk."

He paid no attention to her words, but went on:

"One unbuttons one's self, one reveals one's self. Look at your eyes and your smile. I have felt it in my own eyes: hundreds of times, I have suddenly seen them all naked together round the table."

"In good company, Cordt?"

"Where else?"

"I don't understand that," she said.

"I do not know the people whom you speak of."

"You will be with them this evening, Adelheid."

She shrugged her shoulders discontentedly and tapped her foot on the carpet.

"Adelheid."

She looked at him and her eyes were dark and angry. He took her hand and held it fast in his:

"I have seen it in eyes that were looking at you, Adelheid."

She drew her hand away:

"This is hideous, Cordt!"

She rose and went to the balcony-door. He looked after her and his eyes gleamed:

"Adelheid."

She stood with her back to him, leaning against the window-frame, and buttoned her gloves. He leant forward and gripped the arms of his chair with his hands:

"I have seen it in *your* eyes, Adelheid."

She did not move, uttered not a word. When she had finished buttoning her gloves, she gathered up her train and went out on the balcony.

The May air was cold and she shivered in her thin gown. The lamps shone dimly through the mist; many carriages drove across the square. She could hear the tinkling of the harness-bells in the gateway; the footman was tramping up and down below.

She turned and stood at the window and looked at Cordt. He had moved his chair round towards the fireplace. She could see nothing of him but one shoulder and arm, his thick hair and his legs.

"The carriage is there," she said.

He rose and went to her.

"You must not be angry with me," he said, gently. "I am out of sorts."

"Are you ill?"

"Yes ... perhaps.... No, not that."

"Well, for all that I care, we can stay at home. You have spoilt *my* pleasure."

"Have I?"

"Of course you have. It was for you I made myself look so nice ... it was with you I wanted to go out."

"Was it?"

He took her hand and drew her to the fire:

"Sit down, Adelheid ... there ... only for a minute. Shall we stay at home to-night ... get some wine ... have a party of our own...?"

"Yes ... you're in such a festive mood!"

"Now be good, Adelheid. You are my only dissipation.... You know you are ... there have been hundreds of delightful days to prove it. If you are of my mind to-night, we will do this. And you will be beautiful for me and I for you and our eyes will sparkle together."

She did not look at him, but shook her head:

"I will stay at home, if you wish it," she said.

They sat silent. The candles on the mantelpiece flickered and guttered in the draught.

"It is strange," he said. "Do you remember the evening in London, Adelheid, when we were to go to that great ball? Then I begged you to stay at home and you did and you were glad."

She lay far back in her chair, with her arms behind her neck:

"I was not glad that evening," she said.

He raised his head and listened.

"I submitted, Cordt, but I was not glad to. I was acting a part, for your sake."

She met his eyes. Hers were still and sad and she did not remove them while she spoke:

"I was wicked, Cordt. I hated you. I told you a lie. I was dancing at the ball, hour after hour, while I sat and held your hand and laughed so gaily."

She slipped from her chair and crouched before him, with her hands folded round his knee and her eyes fixed humbly on his face:

"Do not look at me so strangely, Cordt. That is how I am. I love you. But I cannot live without the others ... without having them to see it, to see my happiness. I want to be pretty and I want them to fall in love with me and I want to belong to you. I only care to be pretty if I am loved. Don't look like that, Cordt."

She clung to him with eyes of entreaty.

"I am not really wicked, Cordt ... am I? I was with our little baby day and night when he was ill ... wasn't I, Cordt?"

"Yes," he said.

"Yes ... I was. But I cannot always be quiet."

He lifted her from her chair and crossed the room with his arm round her waist. They went out on the balcony. A carriage came across the square at a brisk trot, followed soon after by a multitude of others. They came from the streets all round, but drove away in the same direction and disappeared round a street-corner. The horses' hoofs clattered against the pavement, the lamps shone on the glittering carriages, coachmen and footmen sat stiff and black on their boxes.

"Come, Adelheid," he said. "Let us go."

The candles on the mantelpiece burnt down and the faces in the big chairs grinned in the darkness. When day dawned, the old servant came and arranged the room. When it was evening, he lit the candles.

He did this the next day and the next and many days after. The sun rose and the sun set. The water splashed in the fountain. The lamps shone and the people swarmed over the square. The balcony was bright with its red flowers and, every evening, the light fell through the open door.

But the summer passed and no one entered the room.

CHAPTER III

Fru Adelheid stood on the balcony. She plucked the red flowers and threw them into the square below. She wore a long, white gown; her gloves and her white boa lay on the ground. She had just come from the theatre and had been bored.

Now she turned towards the room.

Cordt sat huddled together before the fireplace and stared in front of him. She wanted to see his face and called to him. He pushed back his chair and looked up:

"I was thinking of the play we have been to see," he said.

"Yes, it was stupid."

She drew the other chair over the floor, so that she could look at the jar with the naked man writhing through thorns.

"There was a time when I was tired of law," said Cordt. "I was glad when the poet showed me a marriage that was broken for love. I used to think that people grew greater through it and that Heaven seemed higher and earth more green."

She shuddered again and wrapped her skirt closer about her feet.

"Now I am so tired of lawlessness. I loathe these women and their lovers."

"You are married yourself now," she answered.

"What do you say?"

He looked up. She could see that he had not caught her words and she was glad.

"There must be a struggle, no doubt," she said.

"Of course there must. There is. In the old days, they were not allowed to come together and now they are not allowed to stay together."

She said nothing, but let her hand glide over the jar.

"All these faithless wives have lowered love. I could imagine a woman of refinement stifling her love, because she would not give it scope."

"Because she was afraid."

"Because she was refined."

They sat silent for a time and looked at the live embers in the white ashes.

"Do you think there are many who do that?"

He looked up.

"Do you think there are many faithless wives?"

"I don't know. Why shouldn't there be?"

He leant his head on his hands. Fru Adelheid played with the jar.

"But I can't understand that people care to go to the theatre."

"Where would you have them go?"

He pushed back his chair so that he could see her. She remained sitting as she sat and thought of nothing.

"Adelheid," he said, "I suppose you wouldn't care to stay at home to-night?"

She lay back in her chair and looked at her hands.

"Oh," she said, "I wanted to go out to supper."

"I should so much like to talk to you."

"But I did come home from the theatre, dear," she replied and put out her hand to him.

He did not see it and she let it fall.

"I would rather have stayed at home after the theatre, Adelheid."

"Yes, I see," she answered and just shrugged her shoulders. "I did not understand."

"But you understood it in the theatre. And now you want to sup out all the same."

He bent over to her to catch her eyes. She said nothing and did not look at him.

"Adelheid."

Fru Adelheid knit her brow:

"I don't go to the theatre, you see, for the sake of the play," she said. "That does not amuse me. But it amuses me to watch that sea of people and to hear them clamor and then fall silent. I like the way they clap and the way they are quite still when anything good is being said on the stage. Then something sings inside me and I enjoy it."

He looked at her for a moment; then he laughed and rubbed his hands. Fru Adelheid turned her chair towards him, so close that her knees touched his:

"What is it that you wanted to talk to me about this evening?" she asked. "That couldn't be postponed until the theatre was over? That couldn't wait for an hour, now that I feel like going out to supper?"

He looked at her and shook his head.

"*Was* it anything? Or were you only tired and empty, as I was ... and as the faithless wives are ... and the modern poets and ... and everybody?"

"No, Adelheid," he said. "No. It was nothing. Nothing at all."

"I don't know what you mean," she said and suddenly flung herself violently back in her chair. "There is something behind your words."

Cordt nodded.

"You are angry with me. What is it that I do? We live no differently, that I know of, from other people in our circle. We travel, we go to the theatre, we go out and we receive our friends at home. We meet amusing people, artists ... everybody who is anybody."

"Are you always amused among amusing people?"

She looked at him a little doubtfully:

"There is no such thing as always anywhere."

"No," he said, "more's the pity. There is not."

They sat silent, both steeped in thought. Then he pushed his hair from his forehead and said, calmly:

"Try if you can understand me, Adelheid. When a woman marries and becomes a mother, she usually becomes quiet ... quieter, I mean. I mean that there are victories which she cannot win, triumphs which she cannot achieve ... which she does not trouble about. She does not trouble about them, Adelheid, because she has deepened her life ... because she has come so near to one man that the approach of other men is distasteful to her. Then she becomes quiet ... quieter. And this quietness is not empty, but just richer than all the rest."

She looked at him with a strangely inquisitive flash in her angry eyes:

"Are you jealous?" she asked.

He shook his head and made a gesture of denial with his hand. But she sprang from her chair and stood before him with great, proud eyes:

"You ought to be, Cordt," she said. "You ought to be. I am yours and I love you. You won me once: see to it that you know how to keep me. Fight for me, Cordt. I am young, I am pretty and the world is full of men."

He rose deliberately and looked at her till she thought for a moment that he would strike her.

"You will be twenty-six next month," he said. "And, besides, we in our family don't fight to keep our wives."

"Cordt."

She sat down without knowing what she was doing. He looked at her and she looked back at him. She could not help thinking how tall he was; and how easily he wore his clothes; and that one of his shoulders was a little lower than the other.

Then he crossed the room, so quickly that he nearly tripped over the carpet. He struggled with the old spinning-wheel and pulled it over the floor. She followed him with her eyes.

"Can you spin on my great-grandmother's wheel, Adelheid?" he asked.

She crossed her arms on her breast and looked at him.

"Can't you, Adelheid? Couldn't you learn? Not if I begged you to?"

He pulled the spinning-wheel right in front of her and placed it as if she were to use it then and there. Then he sat down in his chair again.

"Don't you think you could, Adelheid?"

They looked hard at each other. Then they became timid and shy and dropped their eyes.

They both thought of holding out their hands, but neither could see the other's. They longed to throw themselves into each other's arms, but they sat as stiff as statues. Their lips trembled; but they did not look at each other and neither knew anything of the other's thought.

"I am thinking how very small we look in these big chairs," he said, at last.

His voice was calm and she grew quite calm at once. It was all over; there was peace in their souls. It was not a reconciliation, for they remembered no quarrel. Their glances rested confidently upon each other.

There was nothing between them and they were friends.

"I wonder if we are inferior to those who sat here before us," she said. "Different, yes; but inferior?"

They both rose.

"Much inferior," said Cordt, "and much less happy."

They crossed the room and went out on the balcony, as was their custom before they went to bed.

The stars of the September night rode in a high sky. Most of the lamps were extinguished and there were but few people in the square. A drunken man was singing far away. The sound of the water falling in the fountain swelled up in the silence.

"How beautiful it is here!" he said.

"Yes."

"And now the summer nights are over and we have not enjoyed them."

She laid her head on his shoulder and closed her eyes.

"I do not think that in the whole world there is a square so pretty as this," he said.

"Oh, yes ... in Florence...."

He sighed and led her into the room:

"We have travelled too much, Adelheid."

She crossed the floor quickly and opened the door. He remained standing on the balcony.

It had all seethed up in him again. He fought against it, but to no purpose.

"Are you coming, Cordt?"

She was outside in the passage and could not see him.

"Do you go.... I will come presently."

He forced his voice to be as calm as possible, but it sounded very unnatural in his own ears. He stood quite still and listened. She remained standing for a moment, as though she were considering.

Then she closed the door and went. He could hear that she went hurriedly.

CHAPTER IV

The first snow had fallen and lay fine and white on the balcony, embroidered by the feet of the sparrows.

The red flowers stood indoors, in the warmth, and looked pitiful. And a big table had been placed at the back of the room, with a lamp upon it and a pile of books.

Cordt came early.

He went straight up to the table, sat down and opened a book. Soon after, he stood at the window and looked out.

It was growing dusk. A damp and misty evening, with a thin, reddish light behind the mist and cold feet and dripping roofs. The snow on the square had melted into slush. The fountain was silent, covered with boards and pine-faggots.

He sat down again and read. He stood up, looked at his watch, went to the window, walked up and down the floor and sat down again. He lit a cigar and let it go out. He went away and came back in an hour and began all over again.

A little before midnight, the carriage drove in through the gateway and, five minutes later, Fru Adelheid stood in the room, tall and white, with large eyes.

"Have you enjoyed yourself, Adelheid?"

She could hear that he did not care to know and she did not answer:

"I am freezing," she said.

She drew her chair close up to the fire, nestled into it and put her feet on the fender.

"They asked after you, Cordt."

"I daresay."

He turned over the leaves of his book a little, then closed it and drew his chair beside hers. He sat resting his cheek in his hand and looked tired.

"Do you intend to sit in this room all day, Cordt?"

"No, only in the evening. When I have nothing else to do. I love this room."

She pressed her hands hard together and closed her eyes.

"I hate it," she said. "All the unkindness that has come between you and me comes from here."

He said nothing to this, but rose and went to the table for a cigar. Something went through her as he slammed the lid of the box.

"Are you going with me to-morrow?"

He shook his head.

"Do you want to cut off all our acquaintance, Cordt?"

"No," he said. "I do not. But I don't care to go out just now."

"What do you think our friends will say?"

"Let them say what they like."

"Don't you consider how unpleasant it is for me?"

"Oh, yes. But I don't care to go out at present."

He lit his cigar at the candle on the mantel-shelf. Then he sat down again and smoked quietly and looked into the fire. She looked at him and sighed.

And, without knowing how it happened and without intending it, she suddenly felt her heart touched and her eyes grew moist:

"Are you not happy, Cordt?"

He looked up and gazed at her:

"No."

"And it is my fault? Because your wife is a silly woman, who wants to go out every day?"

"You are not that, Adelheid."

"Because I am an empty, restless, modern creature?"

"You are not that."

"What am I then, Cordt?"

He took her hand and kissed it and smiled to her:

"You are my wife, Adelheid. And we have a little baby, we two, and perhaps will have another."

"No," she said and drew her hand away. "No, Cordt. That was only my nonsense."

He said nothing. His hand fell down slackly and he turned paler than she could remember ever having seen him. She was afraid that he was ill and stooped over him and called to him.

He did not see her, did not hear her.

She could not take her eyes from him. She thought he could not look more distressed if their boy were dead. She felt it as an appalling shame, that she herself was glad of it; and she dreaded lest he should look at her.

Then he did and read her thoughts.

And she grew worse and worse the more she saw him grieve. She did not understand it, felt troubled by it.

And, as there was no anger in his eyes, it grew worse for her still. She cast about for a word that could make him move and say something, no matter what.

But he sat still and silent and slowly turned his face away from her. And she could find nothing to say.

She rose and went to the window and stood there for a while. Then she came back and sat down in a chair:

"What are you thinking of, Cordt?"

"Of you."

Again they sat silent.

"Adelheid."

He spoke her name quite calmly and gently, but she was frightened.

"I will fight for you, Adelheid; I mean to fight for you; and the new little baby would have helped me. Now I shall have to fight alone."

She remembered vaguely that this phrase had once been uttered between them, but she did not understand him.

"I will stake life and happiness to win you," he said. "I will talk to you and importune you and conquer you. I will take you in my arms and close my door against you and run after you and forgive you."

"And, if you don't win me?"

"I shall win you."

"But *if*?"

She looked at his mouth, while she listened for the answer. It came quite calmly; he did not even look at her:

"Then I shall cast you off."

Fru Adelheid closed her eyes tightly and then opened them wide:

"Better cast me off at once, Cordt. If you can."

"I can't. We have the baby. And we are fond of each other."

"I don't know," she said.

"What don't you know?"

She did not answer, only shook her head.

"You shall have your liberty," he said. "Go out as much as you please, amuse yourself, fill the house with guests. Be gay and melancholy the whole day long, as your fate decides. Go away, if you feel inclined."

"And will you never go with me?"

"As little as possible. I will not fight for you out there. I won you there once and I am not afraid for you ... that way. There, in any case, I need not trouble to win you again."

"And then?"

"Then you will know that you can find me here any evening. Here is where I shall live."

He rose and walked slowly through the room. Fru Adelheid let herself slip to the floor and lay there with her cheek on the fender and stared before her. She saw him return and stand beside her and go and come back again.

"Cordt," she said, "I shall never come here."

"You can do about that as you please."

He sat down and rested his head on his hand:

"My ancestor well knew what he was doing, when he built this sacred nuptial secret chamber in his rich, new house ... high above the street, far from the day's work ... and the night's. He saw deep and far."

"It is the torture-chamber of the house," said Fru Adelheid. "I am certain that many women have wept bitterly in here."

He half rose in his seat and passed his hand over his forehead.

"I am frightened, Cordt. You want to ill-use me. I can't do what you wish. Shall we talk somewhere else ... in your room, Cordt?"

"No," he said. "Our place is here. Here we are bound to be."

He stood up and sat down again at once. His eyes glittered as he spoke:

"Here they all sat, the men who lived in the house and their wives ... in joy and in sorrow. Their faces look at us from every corner, their words whisper all around.... Can you not hear my great-grandmother's spinning-wheel?... Do you not hear the spinet singing?"

"Yes, Cordt."

"Here our words become greater and weightier in the stillness. Here we grow more powerful in our affection and our anger. Whatever we can do we can do here. They knew something, those old, big men and women."

She rose and stood before him, leaning against the mantel, tall and white:

"They knew how to keep discipline in their house," she said.

She looked at him and there was pride and fear and anger about her red mouth and in her strange eyes.

"That they did," he said. "God bless them for it in their graves!"

She sat down in the old chair and put her arms around the jar, where the man writhed through thorns. She stared at the man's face and it was as though she were with him and felt the thorns in her flesh.

"Here also it was that we two bound ourselves to each other for good and all, Adelheid. That evening when we put our names to the old yellow paper there, in the wall. Then you pledged yourself to this room, which you hate. And, when the time comes, our son will come here with the woman who shall be his joy."

He went out on the balcony and came back, white and wet with snow. He brought the cold in with him and she shivered. He stood silent by the fire and then began to walk about again. She listened to his step and waited for a word and could find nothing to say.

Then she went to the old spinet and sat down and sang:

> My Lenore, how dark and drear
> The burden of daylight's bringing!
> No music of chiming hours I hear,
> No birds in the sunlight singing.
>
> Sweet Lenore, O lady mine,
> Bright-eyed, as the day wanes weaker,
> Now pledge me deep in the golden wine

Night pours from her fragrant beaker.

The violets watch us, blue in the plain,
Not a star our secret misses.
Kiss me, Lenore, and kiss me again
And give me a thousand kisses

The slender tones sang through the room, when she stopped.

She listened, but could not hear his footstep. He was sitting in one of the big chairs and did not move.

She looked at him for a moment over her shoulder. Then she rose and closed the instrument, with as much noise as she could:

"Good-night, Cordt."

"Good-night."

Then she turned very red and very pale and went away with moist and angry eyes.

CHAPTER V

Fru Adelheid was icy cold and had drawn her chair as near the chimney as she could.

It blazed and flared in there; the red glow scorched her face and her white gown. But she kept on adding logs to the fire and could not get warm.

Cordt sat in the other chair reading, with his book on his knees and his head leaning on his hands. The book was a large one, with yellow pages and old-fashioned characters.

Fru Adelheid looked at him despondently. She regretted that she had come up to the room and would have gone away, had she had the strength to. She sighed and looked into the fire with tired eyes.

"Adelheid ... listen."

He pushed his hair with both hands from his forehead and read:

> "But, when the tidings came to Queen Thyre that Olav Trygvasson was dead, she fell into a swoon and lay thus for long. And, when, at the last, she came to herself again, she was so sorrowful that it was pity for those of her house to behold. When the day was over, she went to a monk who dwelled near by and was known in all that land for a holy man. Him she asked if folk who died by their own hands sinned against God's law; since her lord and husband was dead and she had no more liking for life. But the monk answered and said:
>
> "'Indeed it is a sin. For God has given us life and will take it back again when He thinks right.'
>
> "Then the queen wept, because she must sin so grievously. But, early the next morning, she came again and asked the holy man how little one was allowed to eat without angering God. And the monk took pity on her and said:
>
> "'If you eat an apple every day, that will be enough.'
>
> "Then Queen Thyre lay down on her couch and bade all her handmaidens leave her, so that she might be alone

> with her dule and sorrow, bidding them that one of her maidens, whom she best loved, was to bring her each morning an apple in the golden cup from which she was wont to take her morning draught. And so it fell that, when the maiden came on the morning of the ninth day with the apple in the golden cup, the queen was in Heaven with her husband."

He closed the book; his lips moved as though he were repeating the words to himself. Fru Adelheid looked thoughtfully into the fire. Then she said:

"It was all very well for those old, dead people. They always had a holy man to whom they could go in their distress."

But Cordt shook his head.

"You distort the chronicle, Adelheid," he said. "It was not at all like that. The queen wanted to die and she died. She went to the monk to be released from sin and piously subjected herself to his command."

"They had God, in those days," said Fru Adelheid.

"Yes, they had. The old, strong God held them in His hands."

He rose quickly and stood by the chimney.

"Do you believe in God, Cordt?"

"No," he answered. "I do not. But I believe that He once existed. And I think that it would be a good thing if He were here now."

"I think so too."

He put his foot on the fender and folded his hands over his knee:

"God is somewhere still. And I do not fear His mighty face. If ever I come to look upon it, then I daresay I shall see all that was high and glorious for me in my days, all that made my blood red and my back straight."

Fru Adelheid smiled:

"Is that the old, strong God, I wonder?"

He glanced at her face, but there was nothing there to rouse his anger. Then he crossed the room and stood beside her again with the same expression in his eyes:

"The old, strong God," he said. "I myself can do well enough without Him. But I need Him in my house."

She laid her head back in her chair and laughed:

"Yes, indeed, Cordt. That you certainly do."

And she kept on laughing and said again:

"Then I daresay that wouldn't have happened with ... what was his name, who robbed you down below, in the counting-house? Do you think so, Cordt? And then your wife would kiss your hand every morning and ask to know her stern lord's commands."

He walked up and down and did not answer.

Fru Adelheid understood that he paid no attention to her sally, because her words were too small for his thoughts and she was displeased with herself and angry with him:

"But, to come back to the story, surely there are also Hagbarth and Signe," she said. "Not to speak of Romeo and Juliet. And Maria Veczera ... and Elvira Madigan."

Cordt continued his walk.

"I don't say anything against it. It is a beautiful story. And perhaps it is true besides. In any case, it is right to place a good example before the young. But, as for Queen Thyre, it surely depends a little upon how long she had been Fru Trygvasson."

He did not so much as look at her. She felt that she was being treated as a child whom one does not trouble to answer and she worked herself up into a steadily increasing passion and sought for words to wound him:

"Every love passes," she said. "That we know. It is all very well for those who die first. They show up prettily in history; but there is nothing to prove that they were better than the rest of us."

Cordt was still walking. Now he stood over by the window and looked out. Then he began to walk again

"Cordt."

He stopped before her chair and looked at her.

"Do you know how long King Olav and Queen Thyre were married?"

"What is the point of all this, Adelheid?"

She pushed back her chair and stood up. She was not able to say at once what she wished, but took a step towards him and sat down again and felt quite powerless.

Then there was something in his glance that helped her. And she drew herself up and looked him firmly in the face:

"It means that you are sitting here and growing musty in old books and old stuff and nonsense, while life is taking its course around you. In time, your beard will grow fast to the table and you will never speak a word, except once every ten years, and then it will be so wise and deep that no one will understand it."

"There is no danger of that, Adelheid," he said.

"But I don't want to be Queen Thyre or Signe or any of them," she said; and her voice was so hard that something gave a wrench inside him. "I want to be the woman I am, the woman you fell in love with and took in your arms. I am not in a book. They will never read about me in the girls' schools. I have no time to spare for this endless old drab affection beyond the grave. I don't understand it, I don't believe in it. I want the wild, red love...."

Cordt had turned his face from her, while she was speaking. Now he looked at her again:

"Haven't you got it, Adelheid?"

She lay back in her chair and gave him a strange look. He had never seen those eyes before. Veil after veil fell over them, till they were quite dark, and then there suddenly lighted in them a gleam that was gone at the same moment and the veils fell again.

"I do not know," she said.

She said it so softly that he could only just hear. He listened a moment whether she would say any more.

Then he bowed his head, so that his thick hair fell over his forehead, and threw it back again and turned very pale:

"Indeed?" he said.

He slowly crossed the room to the window and stood with his forehead against the panes. And slowly Fru Adelheid turned her face to him and back again to the fire.

It did not seem to her as though she had said it; and then, the next moment, she heard his quiet answer and saw his face, which was so terribly stern and white. She knew that it was not what she meant to say and she knew that it was true. She felt a bitter remorse at having hurt the man she loved, a senseless despair at not being able to make amends.

Then all this was dissolved in anger that he had led her on to speak like that. And the anger died away in a profound, soft pity for herself.

She saw deeper into her own soul than she had ever done before and turned dizzy with what she saw. She was seized with a wild and curious longing and bent lower over the well. Then it seemed to her as though she were falling and she gripped the arms of the chair so tightly that her knuckles turned white.

And behind the terror was the distant bird, that sang ... a green and golden land, which she had never seen in her dreams....

Cordt stood before her and put out his hand:

"Good-night, Adelheid," he said.

She sat straight up and looked at him in bewilderment:

"Are you going?" she asked.

"No. But I should like you to go to bed. I shall stay here a little longer and read."

He sat down and took his book. Fru Adelheid rose slowly and went across the room.

At the door, she stood for a moment and looked at him. His face was very still. It seemed to her as though he were far away. She wondered whether he would look up and say good-night once more. Or only nod.

But he was reading and turning the pages of his book.

CHAPTER VI

The fire in the hearth was nearly out and the candles had burnt quite low. It was quiet in the room and quiet outside.

Cordt sat in his chair. He had been sitting there long and had not stirred, only pondered, with his fingers buried in his hair, and listened for Fru Adelheid's footsteps.

She was at home, had been at home the whole week. But she had not set foot in the room for the last fortnight.

Cordt looked at his watch. Then he rose and left the room, left the house.

A little later, Fru Adelheid came.

She remained standing at the door, surprised to find the room empty. She called to the balcony, but no one answered. Lingeringly, she went to the window and looked out. There was no one there.

She turned quickly to go. Then the thought came to her of what it had cost her to come up here; and she was annoyed that Cordt was not there. But that was only for a moment; then she was happy again at escaping the encounter. She felt in a lighter mood than she had for many days.

She looked about her curiously. She had never been alone in the room and she seemed not to have seen it properly before.

She stood long in front of the old chairs, lost in contemplation of the strange faces in the woodwork. She pushed them round the floor, placed them opposite each other and beside each other and sat down in them as though to try what it was like. She summoned up in her memory all that she knew about those who had sat in them and amused herself with imagining what one had said and the other.

Then she went to the celestial globe and looked at it. She pressed the spring, so that the stars ran and shone. She looked with delight at the queer plaything and, when the clockwork stopped, set it in motion again.

She pulled out the old spinning-wheel and sat down beside it and set it going. The wheel whirred lustily in the silent room and its whirring put

Fru Adelheid in a very cheerful mood. She wished the great-grandmother would come in at the door and praise her for being so industrious.

She rose from the spinning-wheel and stood in the middle of the room and looked round. She thought of an occasion when she had stood in an Indian temple and reflected that she was examining these singular old things just as calmly as she had contemplated the Hindu sanctuary.

It seemed to her as though she were standing in a mortuary chapel, where old and interesting, but foolish ideas and preposterous superstitions stared at her from the sunken faces of mummies. She felt no terror, for she knew that all that was dead and gone and could never return.

Her eyes fell on the light stain on the wall, where the portrait had hung.

"Poor Fru Lykke!" she said, aloud. "You were shut out of the temple, because your husband deceived you."

And she lifted her arms in the air in jubilant gladness that she was born in gentler times and still lived and felt the warm blood beating in her heart.

Fru Adelheid went round the room and laughed aloud to think how easily she had broken the spell of the old room. She patted the big chairs on their stiff backs and talked kindly to them. She used to hate them; her blood had turned to ice each time she sat in them. Now they were two handsome, valuable chairs and nothing more.

She had torn the veil from the Holy of Holies. There was nothing behind it.

She ran to the window and pulled the curtain aside with a jerk.

There sat the doll ... stiff and stupid.

She laid her face on its waxen cheek and kissed it with her red mouth.

Humming a tune, she sat down to the old spinet. She sought for a hymn that should celebrate her victory over the ghost.

But, when she struck the first notes, she suddenly grew frightened.

She had an uncomfortable feeling that there was some one in the room.

She sprang up, so that the chair upset, and looked around her.

There was no one.

The candles were all burnt out but one and it was dark in every corner. Now the last candle flickered up and struggled a little and went out.

And then there came a treacherous and threatening muttering and whispering all round the room.

People passed over the floor ... many and heavy footsteps. The spinning-wheel whirred, the spinet sang behind her back. The stars ran and shone, the doll rocked at her. The faces in the old chairs raised themselves on their long necks and pecked at her and grinned uncannily.

But the man who writhed through thorns called for help.... She could hear him call. He grew bigger ... he came nearer.... She saw the blood drip from his naked limbs....

Fru Adelheid crept to the door with quivering hands and fearful eyes.

CHAPTER VII

Fru Adelheid laid her hands over Cordt's book:

"May I talk to you a little? May I tell you something? May I tell you that what you are doing is madness?"

He moved her hands from his book and looked up:

"Sit down, Adelheid," he said wearily. "Sit down in that chair."

But she took the book from him and threw it on the floor:

"You are ill, Cordt. You have become ill up here in this dreadful room."

"Have you a household remedy?" he asked.

"How can you have the heart to make a jest of it?"

"It would be a bitter jest, if it were one," he said. "But it was not a jest. I believe in the old household remedies."

Fru Adelheid sat down in her chair and stared helplessly before her:

"Of course you do," she said. "And in old books and in everything that has ceased to exist."

He said nothing, but yawned wearily.

"And God shall be set on His throne again and I shall sit at the spinning-wheel and we shall enjoy a blessed married life and be happy ever after."

Cordt crossed his legs and looked at his nails:

"Yes ... that is my programme," he said quietly. "Something like that. And you have stated it in your usual affectionate manner."

"Cordt, how can you have the heart?"

She swung her body to and fro; her hands lay folded in her lap, her eyes were moist. She wanted to say something, but could not, because the tears prevented her. She could not understand that he did not help her. Then she said:

"Things are going badly with us, Cordt."

And, as he was still silent, she pulled herself together with an effort and spoke with closed eyes, constantly rocking to and fro:

"We must obey the law under which we were born ... must we not, Cordt? After all, we are modern people ... both of us. Tired, empty people, if you like. But we do think and feel otherwise than people did when ... when they were the sort of people whom you like. And we cannot alter ourselves. But we can be as happy as it is possible to be ... nowadays, being what we are. Why should we not be happy, Cordt?"

"I am not happy."

"Oh, Cordt!"

She pressed her hands together and wrung them and bent over them so that her tears fell upon them. Then she turned her wet face to him and asked, softly:

"Then am I no longer pretty, Cordt?"

He stood up and kissed her white forehead:

"That you are," he said. "But that won't help us any longer."

He began to walk up and down. Fru Adelheid wept hard and silently. A little later, she said:

"You are driving me away from you, Cordt. I do so want to tell you this, while there is still time, if only I could find the right words. Won't you sit down a little, Cordt? My head aches so."

He sat down in the chair. Then she rose and put some wood on the fire and sat down again:

"I am so afraid of myself when we talk together, Cordt," she said. "It is not only that I am wicked and say what I do not mean. I do that, too. But you are so good. And you show me thoughts in my mind which are not there before you utter them. But then they come and I think that you are right and that they have been there always. That is so terrible, Cordt."

They sat silent. Fru Adelheid closed her eyes; Cordt moved restlessly in his chair:

"Adelheid," he said.... "You told me that evening...."

"You must not say that ... you must not."

"Do you remember, you said ... about the wild, red love ... that it was not the love which you have?"

She shook his hand and pressed it:

"That is just it," she said. "I am grateful to you because you were so good. And because you did not take it ill. But that was not in me, Cordt. I did not know it. But then you said it ... and made me say ... what I said. But then, at that very moment, I understood that it was so. And that made me feel so terribly bad ... as I did. But then I felt a sort of secret joy ... a secret treasure. It seemed to me that I was richer than before. I was no longer afraid of what may come ... for women sometimes think of that, Cordt, while they are young, how empty everything will be, when that is past."

He listened, with his face turned to the fire.

"I am sure that there is not a man who can understand that," she said.

And then she lay down on the floor, with her chin on the fender ... and her eyes shone:

"A woman is young for so short a time," she said. "And she is always dreading that it will pass. Can't you understand, when she suddenly suspects that there is something greater than the greatest ... and then, when she is sad and afraid ... that then it may suddenly dawn upon her that all is not over yet?"

Cordt laughed:

"It is a poor pleasure to be the greatest when there is something greater still," he said.

But Fru Adelheid shook her head:

"It's not like that, Cordt," she said.

He pushed back his chair and walked up and down many times and it was silent in the room. Then he sat down again beside her and said:

"What you say is true. But it *was* in you and I am glad I showed it to you. I could not do differently, when I once saw it. I cannot go and wait until another man knocks at the secret door of your heart and offers you the greatest of all."

She laid her cheek against the fender and looked at him:

"No, Cordt," she said. "If it is like that, then what I said was not true."

He waved his hand and shook his head impatiently:

"Not to-day or to-morrow," he said. "But in a year, or two years, or ten. And, if it does not happen, then it is only an accident."

Then she moved nearer to him and laid her head on his knee. She looked up to see if he minded. But he was far away in his thoughts and did not notice it.

She suddenly felt peaceful and contented. She was glad that she had got it said. She felt as if it was removed to a distance ... perhaps it was quite gone ... she could not understand why he continued to speak of it.

And what he said about another man seemed so far to her and so impossible. She thought about it as though it concerned somebody else:

"I love you, Cordt," she said. "And, if, one day, another man came and I loved him ... could I help it?"

He sprang up so suddenly that she had to seize the arm of the chair lest she should fall:

"No," he said, scornfully. "You could not."

He rushed through the room and repeated his words three or four times. Fru Adelheid rose from the floor and sat down in her chair and closed her eyes.

"The man who hit upon that excuse did a fine day's work," said Cordt. "He drove out of the world a great portion of men's strength to live their lives."

He threw himself so violently into his chair that Fru Adelheid started. Then he sat long quiet and she was glad that he was silent.

"Why should one not be able to control one's heart?" he said, at last. "Suppose I have a wife and child; and my wife is she whom I myself chose. Then, one day, I meet another woman, who rouses my desires. I meet her at a party, where there are lights and wine and music ... we are not ourselves, she and I ... we are in another mood than usual ... everything is done to lead us from the way by which we go on ordinary days. But why should I not be able to step aside, in loyal gratitude for that which I possess?"

She opened her eyes at intervals and closed them again. She heard what he said, but did not realize that he was speaking to her.

"Who is it that placed love outside the laws? If I take it into my head to kill a fellow-creature, there is no doubt but that I am indulging a most criminal fancy. If I have given my word and think of breaking it, I am no gentleman. But my heart may do as it pleases."

"Yes," said Fru Adelheid.

She was thinking of nothing when she spoke and he did not hear her.

"There are people, we know, who have the right to send thousands to their death," he said. "There are people whose passion rises skywards in red flames and devours the poor chattels that stand in its way and lights up all the land. Poets sing about it and a wax taper burns before its image in every human heart. But, if a man plays the Napoleon in the Store Bröndstræde, we hang him ... Why should every second woman be entitled to look upon herself as an Héloïse?"

He sank into his chair and stared before him:

"I am not sure either whether the radiance of the one great flame makes up for the thousand tiny lights that are put out. Does any one know, I wonder? Can any one measure it?"

Fru Adelheid moved and Cordt turned his face to her and looked at her attentively. Her eyes were soft and dreamy; she smiled faintly, like a drowsy child.

"And *if* that be so," he said, in a subdued voice, "if it be the case that I am not able to control my heart...." He let his head fall heavily on the arm of the chair. "*If* it be the case that love makes me happy and confident, so that I build my life and the life of my family upon it ... if it can then expire, without my knowing how or why, and I have to look for the mother of my children in a strange man's bed, then why do I let my wife go out in the street unveiled? Why do I not lock her up, as the Turk does? Or why do we not kill the mother when the child is born?"

He rose and walked round the room and grew calmer as he walked:

"But it is not so," he said. "Let the great keep their greatness ... let the poets celebrate them and the puny moderns ape them in their wretched way. And may there always be women who cannot give themselves more than once and men who love them."

He stood by the fire and looked through the room. It was still on every side; the church-clock struck two.

"See, Adelheid," he said, "how life passes more and more into law's domain. Every day, the liberty of the one is taken for an encroachment upon the rights of the other. Every day, land, hitherto free of law, is regulated by law. Flowers beget no flowers without the gardener's consent; animals no longer select their own mates. But no one can control his heart; and human beings pair like dogs in the street."

The fire had burnt out when Cordt woke from his musings.

He saw that Fru Adelheid was asleep. He stood before her a long time, sick with compassion for her and for himself.

Then he stroked her gently on the hair:

"It is late ... Adelheid."

CHAPTER VIII

"I could wish we were not married, Cordt," said Fru Adelheid.

She laid her arms across her breast and looked at him with deep, dark eyes:

"I could wish I were your mistress. If it meant that, all would be over and done with in the morning. Then there would be no more of this unpleasantness. And no fear, either. And the joys we have would be all the fairer."

He stood by the fire and played with the keys in his pocket.

"Then your forehead would be smooth and your eyes bright, Cordt, for then you would be making love to me."

He looked up and said gently:

"Don't I make love to you, Adelheid?"

She sighed and said nothing. Cordt sat down in his chair and time passed. Then he asked:

"Do you hear what I say, Adelheid?"

"I am longing to hear what you will say next."

"I read something similar to what you have been saying in a book lately," he said. "I forget what the book was called. I was looking into it ... just where the author railed against marriage, with its security and its habits and all that. I have read exactly the same thing in a hundred books, I think."

"Yes ... they all sing the same song," she replied. "It is not particularly entertaining. But it is true enough, I daresay."

Cordt struck his hands together lightly:

"It is curious how little imagination the poets have nowadays," he said. "One would think there were only half a dozen women, whom they have all kissed and married and run away from. I wonder that it never occurs to one of them to glorify *custom*."

Cordt pulled his chair forward and sat with his head in his hands and looked into the fire:

"If I were a poet, I would sing a song in honour of sacred custom," he said.

"Would you, Cordt?"

"Yes, yes ... that I would."

He laid his head back and listened to the gale whistling in the chimney:

"Now just look, Adelheid, at two people thrown into each other's arms by the strongest power on earth. For them there exists neither day nor night, neither time nor place. The whole earth is fragrant with violets. Their joy is terror and their terror is full of exultant gladness. Then a child lies in her lap and the light in her eyes is deeper than before. And then the years go by ... there are fewer violets on the earth as the years go by, Adelheid. She bears her children in pain. And the pain sears her cheek. The children have sucked her breast dry; her eyes are weary with the night-watches. The stranger who passes the house sees only the faded woman. But he who drank intoxication from her young eyes and kissed the strength of her bosom ... he does not see it. He has grown *accustomed* to that woman. She has quenched the longing of his youth and given him peaceful happiness instead."

He was silent for a while. Then he turned his face towards her:

"He does not live in his first eager longing for the trysting-hour, but confidently seeks his accustomed couch by her side. Custom has gently bound the two people into one family. Is that not beautiful, Adelheid? And good?"

"Yes," she said. "It is beautiful, as you tell it. But it is not youth."

"Then what is youth, Adelheid?"

"Youth is not rest."

"Then one should not marry before one is old," said Cordt. "For marriage is rest. Deep, powerful, happy ... generating rest."

"No more one should," replied Fru Adelheid. "And that is why I could wish I were your mistress."

She looked at him, as she said this, and he at her.

Then he stood up and laid his hand on the back of her chair and bent close down to her:

"How far estranged from each other we have become!" he said.

And Fru Adelheid nodded sadly and Cordt crossed the room and stood by the fire again:

"In vain I pitch my call in every key," he said. "It has availed me nothing that my ancestor built this room ... his heirs have borne witness here, generation after generation, to no purpose."

A gust of wind came and blew the balcony-door open.

Fru Adelheid shuddered and looked that way, while Cordt went and closed it. Then he remained standing by the celestial globe and pressed the spring:

"I so often think of the poor man who placed this toy up here," he said. "He was a man who could not be content with the circle in which he moved. So he lost his reason and devoted himself to playing with the stars.... For us modern people it is different ... the other way round. We go mad because the circle in which we move is too large. We leave the stars to the babies. We play ball with bigger things. We try a fall with God Himself, if the fancy takes us ... provided that we have not outgrown that plaything too! We dare not speak of love and we smile at marriage. We despise courage and do not believe in honesty and each of us has his own opinion about virtue."

She heard what he said even as people listen to music when it does not so very much matter if they catch every note.

"Then it happens that we long for a fixed point in our lives ... just one point. Something that cannot be pulled to pieces and discussed. And something that is not past."

Cordt sat and moved about in his chair and could not settle down:

"If I were to put anything in this room," he said, "it would be a little tiny house ... from far away in the country. There would be only one door and two windows and it would be evening and the smoke would rise up gently from the chimney. The house would have to be as small as could be; but that would show that there was no room for doubt inside it. Husband and wife would go in and out of the door to the end of their days."

Now she heard what he said and looked at him.

"That is what my marriage ought to be, Adelheid. If I had had any talent, I daresay it would have been different. Or if I had to work for my bread.... And I am no different from other men of to-day ... no stronger, no braver. I know nothing about God and I have no excessive belief in men."

He had lowered his voice and spoke without looking at her. But she understood that he was listening for a word from her and her heart wept because she had nothing to say to him.

"My fixed point," he said.

Then he was silent for a little. But, soon after, he rose and stood with his arm on the back of her chair and spoke again:

"There was also something in what I used to see at home. Father and mother were so kind ... and so strong. I see them before me now, as they used to kiss each other after dinner, however numerous the company might be. And they kissed each other good-morning and good-night until they died. And when father and his brother met in the street, they always kissed ... people used to laugh ... and it was such a pretty habit."

While he spoke, she sought for an opportunity to interrupt him.

"My family-feeling has always been too strong," he said. "Until now. And yet ... I once had a sweetheart...."

He stopped. Fru Adelheid sat up and looked at him. Her eyes shone.

"Or a connection, if you like...."

"You never told me about that!" she said.

Cordt raised his head and looked at her and she lowered her eyes.

"There is nothing to tell," he said.

Then he said no more, but went to the window and stood there.

And Fru Adelheid again felt small and ill at ease in the big old chair.

CHAPTER IX

Cordt stood on the threshold and waited, but then closed the door and went to the fire.

He was in dress-clothes and tired and pale and his eyes were bright with wine. When he had been sitting for a little while, it grew too warm for him and he drew his chair to the balcony-door. There he sat and let his hands play with the red flowers.

Fru Adelheid did not see him when she entered.

She moved slowly and stopped in the middle of the room, when she discovered that he was not by the fireplace. She was surprised at this, but soon forgot it, in her gayety and her lingering excitement at the evening's entertainment, with her mind full of bright and clever phrases and the lights gleaming in her great eyes.

She sat down to the spinet and laid her forehead against the keys. Something was singing inside her; her foot softly beat the carpet.

Then she sought among the music and sang:

> Lenore, my heart is wrung.
> Thine is so dauntless, thine is so young.
> Tell me, Lenore, the truth confessing
> (Which never were mine by guessing):
> Whence do thy soul's fresh fountains pour?
> Where the mountains dip or the valleys soar?
> Tell me, the truth confessing;
> Open to me youth's door.
>
> Lenore, my heart is sad.
> Thine is so constant, thine is so glad.
> Teach me thine equable gait to borrow;
> Teach me laughter and sorrow.
> My heart is a desert, sterile and bare;
> My heart is thine: do thou whisper there
> Of a fount that shall flood to-morrow,

Of a sun that shall gild God's air.

She put one hand on the music-sheet and played with the other and hummed the tune again.

Then Cordt clapped his hands in applause. She started and her hand fell heavily on the keyboard:

"How you frightened me, Cordt!"

He came and stood beside the spinet. Fru Adelheid looked at his face and sighed. Then she stood up, put the music away and went and sat in a chair by the fireplace:

"Won't you come here, Cordt?"

Cordt walked to and fro again and up and down.

"Sit down here for a little," she said.

"Why should I?" he asked. "You are not here, you know."

She looked up and met his calm eyes.

"You are still down below, among the crowd of our guests. Don't you know that, Adelheid? They are all empty carriages that drove out at the gate. For, as each one came to shake hands and say good-bye, you entreated him to stay a little longer."

Fru Adelheid sighed and crossed her hands in her lap. He stood up by the fireplace so that he could see her face.

"I was sitting over there among the flowers, when you came in, and I saw it all. You entered with a gleam and a rustle, accompanied by the whole throng ... you were the fairest of them all. By your side went Martens, supple and handsome. A long way after came his wife ... the woman who wears those tired eyes and that painful smile. She did not even look to see to whom he was offering his homage."

She puckered her forehead and looked at him angrily.

"Then he begged you to sing the song once more and they crowded round you and added their entreaties to his. You crossed the floor ... with your slow, sure gait.... You always walk in the same way, Adelheid ... like one who is not to be stopped. Your white dress trailed behind you; there was silence in the room."

Cordt ceased for a moment. Fru Adelheid laid her head back in the chair and closed her eyes.

"Then you sang ... his song ... the one you were singing a minute ago at the old spinet.... Yes, you heard me applauding, Adelheid. He stood beside you and looked at you ... deferentially, happily. And you looked at him to read in his eyes how charming you were."

"How wicked you make it all seem!" she said.

Cordt bent over her:

"Look at me, Adelheid."

She looked at him and was afraid.

"How dare you come up here with your retinue?" he asked. "Up here ... to me ... in this room? Look at me, Adelheid. Is there not room enough in the house besides? Are there not a hundred houses in the town where you can play the game you love?"

Fru Adelheid stretched out her hands to him:

"Cordt!"

But his eyes were large and stern and she could not bear to look into them.

Then she rose and stood before him with bowed head:

"Shall I go, Cordt?" she asked, softly.

He did not answer, but crossed the room. And Fru Adelheid sat down on the edge of the big chair, as if she were not at home in the room.

"Yes ... Martens," he said.

"You were not at all friendly to him this evening, Cordt."

She said this in order to say something and without thinking, but regretted it at the same moment and looked at him dejectedly. But he made a gesture with his hand and answered, calmly:

"Indeed I was. As friendly as he could wish and a great deal more so than I feel."

He stood by the mantel and looked down before him. She took his hand and laid her cheek against it:

"Martens is nothing to me," she said.

"No," said Cordt. "Not really. It is not the man ... it is men. It has not gone so far as that. But it has gone farther."

"I don't understand you," she said, sadly.

"It is not a man, a good man or a bad one, that is wooing your heart and has won or is trying to win it. Martens is not my rival. He does not love you and he is not trying to make you believe that he is. He does not lie. That is not called for nowadays, except among the lower classes. With us, we rarely see so much as the shade of a scandal. Whence should we derive the strength that is needed for a rupture, a separation, a flight from society? It's a soldier that tells his girl that she is his only love ... a journeyman smith that kills his faithless sweetheart ... a farm-girl that drowns herself when her lover jilts her for another."

He drew away his hand and folded his arms across his chest.

"Martens is no Don Juan. It is not his passion that infatuates women, not his manly courage and strength that wins them. He carries his desires to the back-streets; he takes his meals with his wife. He cannot love. The women become his when he covets them, but he has never belonged to any woman. His eyes, his words, his ditties sing love's praises with a charming, melancholy languor which no woman can resist. Then he lays his head in her lap and tells her of his perpetual yearnings and his perpetual disappointments. He unbosoms himself to her and begs her not to betray him. Then she loves him. And she is his ... to any extent he pleases."

She tried to speak; but Cordt shook his head in denial and she sighed and was silent.

"He is no longer young. But that makes no difference. He was never young. His unbounded susceptibility, his eternal readiness make him young in the women's eyes, as though he were a woman in man's clothing. His limp sensuousness has permeated every fibre of his body and his soul ... so much so that it affects his every word, look and thought. He is destitute of will and insipid and sickly and untrustworthy. He is never hungry and he is insatiable. He swallows women and spits them out again ... with morbid longings and a despondent temper and a diminished strength to live their lives."

"Cordt!... Cordt!... What is he to me?... What is he to us?"

He looked at her and was silent for a moment. Then he said:

"Martens tends the garden in which you pluck your flowers. He is the chief gardener. But he is only one of a thousand. In the main, these passion-hunters are all alike. Shall I introduce them to you?"

"No, Cordt."

"I can do so without hurting the feelings of any of them by mentioning their names," he said. "You will recognize them all. You will recognize them at once."

"Cordt!"

But Cordt did not hear.

"You will remember the man of whom we all know that he has many mistresses, even though we can say nothing to his face. He often takes a new one. Then he has one more ... that is all ... for he never lets go the old ones."

"That will do, Cordt."

"Then there is the man who tells his fair friends that he has only loved one woman in his life and that is his mother. Have you ever observed the part which the mother plays in these worn-out men's imaginations? In their books ... in their love ... she is the emblem for their morning head-aches, their impotent compunctions. Her business it is to soothe their worm-eaten thoughts ... they whisper her name while they kiss their lady-loves. I don't know which is the greater insult: that offered to the mother or to the mistress."

Fru Adelheid tried to rise, but just then he passed so close to her that she could not move. So she remained sitting, weary and racked, and he went round the room and stopped here and there while he spoke:

"These are the men to whom our wives belong," he said. "And they do not take them away, so that we can bemoan their loss and get new wives in their stead. They are content to nibble the crest of the tree of love, which we have planted in our garden, and to leave it to stand and thrive as best it can."

Fru Adelheid stood up before him with moist eyes and quivering lips:

"Cordt!"

But Cordt's face was white with anger and she could not find a word to say.

"Do I amuse you, Adelheid?" he asked.

She went to her place by the chimney and sat down again:

"You are putting out all my lights," she said.

He walked across the room and went on talking:

"A man's honest love goes for nothing, when one of these gentry has laid eyes on his wife. Then he is degraded to the mere husband ... a dull and clumsy person ... the owner of something which he cannot own. Then there awakes in my wife's mind a longing for something which she does not possess. Her peace has turned into weariness and the love which her marriage offered into an empty custom. She resigns herself. And the silly words of every silly book sing in her ears. She knows that no love endures for ever ... that marriage is odious. Impatient sighs rise up in her soul, embitter her days and sadden her nights. Then she changes the gold of love for small coin and fritters it away, while the lights shine forth and the music strikes up."

He folded his hands about his neck and stood by her chair and looked before him:

"Adelheid," he said ... "I cannot understand that the men who occasion this state of things are allowed to go free among us. And we honor them as the most distinguished of mankind. When we see a poor cripple, a shudder comes over us ... am I not right, Adelheid? We are disgusted with a face full of pain. But these lepers beam before our eyes with a radiance and a beauty that know no equal."

He walked up and down for a while and time passed and there was silence in the room.

Then he sat down in his chair, where it stood by the balcony-door, among the red flowers.

He was tired and closed his eyes. Now and then, he opened them, when a carriage drove across the square or a cry sounded. Then he closed them again and fell into a drowsiness in which everything was present to him and painful.

And then suddenly he started up.

Fru Adelheid was lying before him on the floor, with her cheek against his knee. His hand was wet with her tears.

"Don't be angry with me, Cordt!"

He looked at her, but said nothing.

"Cordt ... when you speak like that ... it is true ... true for me also.... It is all so good and so beautiful...."

He pushed back his chair and rose to his feet:

"Be very careful what you do, Adelheid," he said. "I am not a fashionable preacher, working up your nerves and quieting them again ... not a poet, reading his last work to you. I am your husband, calling you to account."

He crossed the room and then returned and stroked her hair:

"It is beyond our strength, Adelheid," he said, sorrowfully. "God help us!"

She took his hand and laid it over her eyes, so firmly that it hurt her.

"If the old God were still here, then we could go down on our knees and fold our hands together, as they did who built this room. Would that not be good, Adelheid?"

"Yes."

"I call upon Him, Adelheid.... And upon everything in the world that is greater than my own power.... And upon the little child downstairs...."

CHAPTER X

Fru Adelheid lay on the floor before her chair and pulled the flowers of her bouquet to pieces. Cordt sat with his head leaning on his hand and looked at the flowers.

"If only you would speak, Cordt.... If only you would ask me something. Why don't you ask me something?"

"What can I ask you?"

"Ask me what I am thinking about. Why I have come home so early. Why I have not been here for so long."

"I know all that, Adelheid."

She crossed her hands on her knee and swayed to and fro and looked at him with dark and angry eyes:

"Is there anything you do not know, Cordt?"

"No."

"I don't think so either. You know the right and the wrong of everything between heaven and earth. You are never in doubt and never at a loss. You know at once what is good and what is bad; and then you go away and do what is good."

He shook his head and said nothing and she grew still more angry:

"You alone know. Whoever does not obey you is lost. There is no room in the house for any but you and those who serve you."

Cordt bent over her and lifted her up in the chair.

"Be silent for a little, Adelheid," he said. "And stay quiet for a little."

But she slipped to the floor again and looked at him defiantly:

"I will not sit in that chair," she said. "Never again. I am not worthy of the honor. You do not know everything, Cordt. You do not know me."

He stroked her hair with his two hands and forced her head back:

"Then show yourself to me," he said.

She released her head and her eyes grew moist:

"You must not be good to me," she said. "You don't know me. I am not the woman you think."

Then she laid her head on the chair and said, softly:

"I am so sad, Cordt."

"You will be glad again."

"I daresay," she said. "But I shall always be sad."

She took the ruined bouquet and laid it on the chair and her cheek upon it. She closed her eyes. Cordt looked at her—she seemed so tired—and they were long silent. Then she said:

"It is so cold in here."

And then silence fell upon the room again.

"Cordt!"

Fru Adelheid sat with her back against the chair and stared into the fire with strange eyes:

"Cordt ... do you know ... that sometimes, when I am merriest ... outside ... it is as though I heard little children crying."

He sat silent.

"I hear little children crying, Cordt. When I am dancing ... and sometimes when I am singing. And at the theatre ... when there are many lights and people and I am happy ... then it comes so often. Then I hear little children crying ... far, far away, but still I can hear them distinctly ... I can never help hearing them ... Cordt ... do you know what it is?"

"Yes, I know, Adelheid."

Adelheid looked at him and turned her eyes to the fireplace again:

"Sometimes it happens differently," she said. "When I hear a child crying ... when it is really a child crying ... a strange child, which has nothing to do with me, which I know nothing at all about ... I needn't even see it, Cordt ... but then I have to cry myself."

She was silent for a little. Then she turned her face to him and asked:

"Do you know what that is, Cordt?" And he looked at her calmly and said again:

"Yes, I know, Adelheid."

"I do not know," she said and shook her head softly. "I love our little boy and love to have him with me. Don't I, Cordt?"

"Yes."

"But he is much happier with old Marie. He prefers to be with her. He puts out his little hands to me when I come in. But, when I have had him in my arms for a while, he wants to go back to Marie. He is so small still."

"Yes."

"Sometimes he will not kiss me on any account. He always kisses old Marie."

"When she comes to die, we will put a tombstone on her grave," he said. "And on the stone we will write, *'Here lies one whom the children in the house kissed.'*"

Fru Adelheid folded her hands behind her neck and looked up at the ceiling:

"At one time, you used to tell me about your mother ... that is long, long ago, Cordt. You talked of her so often, in those days ... why do you never do so now?"

"I think only of you."

She moved nearer to him and laid her head on his knee:

"May I lie like this, Cordt?"

He stroked her hair and left his hand lying on her shoulder.

"That's nice," she said.

Cordt looked at her hair and stroked it again. She closed her eyes and nestled up against him:

"It is so quiet here," she said. "Now I will go to sleep."

But then she grew restless again. She half raised herself and lay on her knees, with her hands folded in her lap. Her hair had become undone and slipped down over her shoulders. Her eyes stared into the fire:

"You used to tell me that your mother undressed you every night when you were a little boy," she said. "And every morning she dressed you ... always."

"So she did."

"You said that it so often made her late when she was going to the theatre ... or else she would get up from the table when there were guests. And your father used to be so angry with her."

He nodded.

"I think your father was right," she said. "I think it was odd of your mother ... not quite ... not quite natural."

Cordt pushed the hair from his forehead, but said nothing.

"I could see quite well that you would have me do the same. But I couldn't do it. I can't do it as well as old Marie does and I can't see that that is necessary in order to be a good mother.... Then you also told me that, one evening, when your mother had to go out, you cried without stopping until she came home again."

"Yes."

"But, if your mother had been like me and if old Marie had undressed you every night, then it would have been she whom you would have cried for."

"So it would," he replied. "But it was good for me and good for herself that it was mother."

"I don't understand that," she said.

But then she raised her head and looked at him with great, proud eyes:

"Yes ... I understand," she said. "I understand that it is good for a man and gives him confidence to see his wife chained to her baby's cradle."

"That is so, Adelheid."

He looked at her quietly and sadly and her defiance was broken then and there:

"How strangely you say that," she said. "Cordt...."

Then she laid her head on his knee again and they were silent for a time. Then she said:

"I remember the evening when I was going to my first grown-up ball. A lady came to dress my hair. I was so solemn and the lady so talkative. She told me that I was pretty and that I was sure to be married soon; therefore I must lose no time and dance as much as I could; for, once a girl was married, she had to give up dancing. I asked her what she meant and said that I knew many married women who danced. Then she told me that that was true enough and that there were many fine ladies who did, but then they danced their children dead and therefore it was a great sin."

He moved in his chair. She raised her head and laid it on his knee again:

"Do you believe that we can dance our children dead, Cordt?"

He did not reply, but stroked her cheek. But she pushed his hand away and turned her face and looked at him:

"Do you believe it, Cordt?"

He nodded.

Then Fru Adelheid rose awkwardly from the floor and stood before him. Slowly, she raised her hands and pressed them against her temples.

Cordt sprang up and took her hands firmly in his own and drew her to him. But she tore herself away and her eyes stared vacantly into his and did not see him.

"Adelheid!"

"Those are your children and mine, Cordt ... the little children who cry when I am merry ... the children who died because their mother danced...."

"Adelheid!"

His voice was very soft and his eyes very gentle. She stared into them and saw a gleam in their depths. She understood that he was rejoicing within himself, because he thought that he had her as he wanted her.

He put out his hands to her and his eyes and his silent, quivering mouth spoke a thousand loving words to her. She stood stiff and cold and looked at him stiffly and coldly.

And, when his hands touched her, she drew from him and pushed her chair far back, as if she could not find room enough:

"You do not understand me," she said.

She crossed the room to the balcony-door and stood there. Then she came back to the fireplace, where he had sat down, and looked at him as though he were a stranger:

"Those little children who cry," she said, "what do they cry for?"

He raised his hands and let them fall on the arms of his chair.

"Why do they cry?" she repeated. "Because they have not been brought into a world which is closed to them at the very moment when they see its beauty?... Because they are not born to die?"

She went away again and came back and sat in her chair with a strained expression on her face, as though she had to explain something to one who was slow of comprehension:

"It's no use," she said.

Her voice was harsh. She swung her body to and fro and her thoughts hunted for words in which she could say what she wanted in such a way that it would be settled once and for all and could not be misunderstood.

Then her looks fell on Cordt, as he sat there by her side, shattered and tired, with closed eyes and nerveless hands. She saw the pain she was giving him. She wished to undo and repair it and the tears broke out in her:

"Cordt!"

She took his hand and it lay lifeless in hers.

"Can't you help me?"

"No, Adelheid."

Then her mood changed about. She pushed herself back in her chair and crossed her arms over her breast:

"Then I must help myself," she said. "How could you, either, an old ... yes, an old man like you?"

He did not answer, did not stir, did not look at her.

"An old man like you," she repeated, "who longs for peace and quiet and nothing else. Then you give out that that is the best happiness which is the easiest and the cheapest and the best adapted to domestic use."

Cordt had raised himself upright in his chair. His hands lay clenched about his knee, his eyes blazed.

"Then you put the woman you love in your mother's chair ... your grandmother's and your great-grandmother's chair...."

He flew up and stood before her with his hands on his hips and his lips pressed close together:

"Hold your tongue!"

Fru Adelheid started and looked at him with frightened eyes:

"You have no right to speak to me like that," she said.

He sat down again and threw his head back in his chair, with his face turned away from her. She was so tired, could not find the words she wanted, said everything differently and in another tone than that in which she thought it.

And, as he quieted down beside her, she began to think more clearly than usual and it seemed to her that there was nothing to be done but to say her worst. Then she clenched her fists, to give herself strength, and closed her eyes while she spoke:

"You must know things as they are, Cordt. It is all true, as you have seen it and as you have said it. I have lied to you, Cordt. I lied in my words ... I lied every time I came up here and sat with you."

Now she looked at him. He raised his head with an effort and met her eyes. Then he turned his face away again:

"You are lying now," he said.

She opened her mouth and closed it again, so that her teeth struck together.

Then she crossed her hands in her lap and bent over them and wept:

"I don't know that," she said.

Cordt stood up and walked across the floor, slowly and wearily and without thinking. Fru Adelheid's tears fell into her lap.

They were in this room, each independent of the other, each without sympathy for the other. Their hearts were dead, their thoughts paralyzed. They were no longer two people who loved each other and who strove to be happy, not even two who were angry or sorry because they were to be parted. They were just two people under sentence of death, whom chance had imprisoned in the same cell, but who had nothing else in common.

Cordt was the first to come to his senses.

He was standing behind her chair and the scent of her hair awakened him. He bowed deeper over her and remembered who she was. He looked at her hands, which were wet with tears, and his heart wept with her.

Then, at that moment, he saw that he must spare his sympathy if he wished to keep her. And, when he saw this, he at once realized that she was lost to him for ever.

He sat down in his chair and sought for the words which he should say. He felt like the actor who has to deliver the last sentence in the play, while the audience is already leaving, because the end of the performance is there and the tension over.

"Adelheid!" he said.

That was all he could say. She understood what was passing within him and was speechless too and wept softly.

And the night sped on.

She was lying on the floor again, where she had lain before, with her cheek upon his knee. She talked ... hastily, by fits and starts, without troubling what she said, as long as she could get it all said.

Cordt leant his head on his hand and his thick hair fell over his forehead. He closed his eyes and opened them again, heard what she said and forgot it again, answered from time to time and knew only that it was over.

"There are other men for me besides yourself ... it is true ... it is all true.... Ah, Cordt, may I say it, wicked as it is?... And you will be kind ... you understand that it is not that ... that it is not infidelity...."

She pressed her hands together and shook her head in despair:

"Yes ... yes ... it is infidelity, Cordt ... it is.... It is, because it's you ... and because I understand it now. May I tell you, Cordt ... may I?... I love the desire in their eyes.... I am curious about it.... There is nothing in it that insults me.... I am happy in it, I even try to kindle it...."

"Those things are not said to one's husband, Adelheid."

She looked at him:

"To whom shall I say them, then?"

"Those things are not said."

"Ah ... well ... I say them. I will say them. Because you are the man you are. And, also, you asked me about it, Cordt ... you saw it and wanted to save me ... that was why you spoke to me about it, wasn't it?... I did not know what it was ... now I do know.... I am not lying now ... but I did not know, before you said it. And it is no uglier for me ... it is better for me.... Cordt, Cordt ... it is less ugly so."

She hid her face in her hands and wept so that she could not speak:

"And it is worse still, Cordt ... it is worse than I have said ... why do you not turn me out?... Ah, if you were only dead, Cordt!... Why should you be so unhappy and why should it be I that make you so? If you cast me away, it will be only what I deserve. For I know that it is you I love.... I know it now as I never knew it before ... you are the man that was destined for me...."

She seized his clothes with her hands and half raised herself, so that her white face was close to his:

"Cordt ... can't you wait for me?... I am coming...."

Then she released her hold and sank in a heap on the floor:

"No ... no ... I cannot do what you wish."

He rose to his feet and stood before her and looked into the fire:

"It's your will that is sick, Adelheid," he said.

He walked across the room and stood at the balcony-door and looked out. Then he came back and sat in his chair again:

"You know where the great joy lies. And you know that it would be yours and mine, if you could reach it. But you cannot. There is no sense of perspective in your life ... everything to you seems quite close or quite far, quite small or quite big. You are like Martens and the others. You belong to them, because your will is weak, like theirs. You are becoming like them."

"No, Cordt."

"Yes, you are like them. You are a woman and you are refined and therefore you dread the mire. But you belong to them. You and I are mortal enemies. If you were she whom my son had chosen for his wife, I should tremble for his happiness. And you had the happiness which you seek ... nay, the happiness that exists. You set the cup to your lips when you were young enough to stand wine and old enough to know that it was good."

He pushed the hair from his forehead and looked round the room:

"There is nothing more to be said. You are a child of the time and the time claims you as its own. There was no sense in bringing you to the old room."

"No, Cordt."

"But you are clever and you are refined and you have seen its great, silent beauty. And, one day, you will see that happiness lay in the land where you were and you sallied forth to find it in distant climes."

"Yes, Cordt."

"You will see that, one day. But then it will be too late. Then the years will be gone. Then the strings of the old spinet will be rusted and mute and the spinning-wheel will have fallen to dust and the fire died out in the chimney. Then your fancy will be frightened and bewildered, like the bird that keeps on flapping against the window-pane. Your faith will be lost and your modesty turned to unchastity."

He rose and went across to the balcony-door. Fru Adelheid lay with her cheek on the fender and with closed eyes.

A silence hung over the room greater than it had ever known before. They both of them felt it and felt it as the silence when pain is dumbed at the approach of death. They no longer fought against the inevitable, against what was stronger than themselves; and they were so tired that they no longer thought of the defeat which they had suffered, but only smiled in the peace which they had won.

And the night sped on.

They were sitting again in the quaint old chairs and looked at the embers that were expiring in the hearth. The candles were nearly burnt out.

They were both of them very gentle and very still. It seemed years since they had last differed. Their faces were calm, their eyes clear and sad, when they looked at each other, but without longing, without anger or bitterness.

And they looked at each other and talked together ... of that which was over.

Their words had lost all sting. He held her hand in his and pressed it as that of a good friend. Once, she pushed his hair from his forehead as she would have done to a child.

"If any one saw us sitting here, he would not understand what has happened to us," said Cordt.

"No."

"And, if anyone had heard every word that fell between us in this room, he would perhaps say that we were a pair of simpletons."

Fru Adelheid shook her head:

"It is well that nothing more has happened to us," she said.

"I don't know," replied Cordt.

Then he let go her hand and drew himself up in his seat:

"Sometimes I think it would be easier if there were an action that had to be forgiven," he said. "Something to be forgotten. Then it would not be over."

"It is not over," she said. "We have missed happiness, because I did not keep the measure by which I should be gauged. But our boy down below lives and he can win a wife who shall sit in the old room with honor."

"No," said Cordt. "The secret of the old room is out. It does not suit these times and still less the times to come. Our son shall not see his happiness shattered here."

And, a little later, he pressed his hand hard to his temples and said so softly that she just heard it:

"For it is hard to decrease one's own happiness."

The candles went out ... one after the other.

"It is late, Adelheid," he said. "We had better go."

"Yes," she said.

But neither of them was able to.

They looked at each other and sat steeped in the same thoughts, afraid to end this still night, which was to be followed by bad days.

Then the last candle went out.

Cordt's lamp still burnt on the table, but it was as though everything in the room was displaced in its glow. There was darkness where light had been before and great shadows on the wall.

They both felt it as something uncanny and involuntarily moved closer together.

"Sing to me, Adelheid," he said.

She went to the spinet and sat down and looked at the keys.

"Sing the last of the Lenore songs."

She looked over her shoulder, but could not see the expression on his face.

Then she sang:

> When death comes, come, Lenore, too:
> Thou wert Life's beacon rosy-red;
> And, by those glad, great eyes shot through,
> In that same instant, Death were dead.
> So am I never Death's, but thine;
> No tears shed I, nor once complain:
> Set only thy red lips to mine
> And take thy soul again.
>
> I shall have seen for the last time
> The radiant, loving eyes I treasure;
> And what of song and what of crime
> I wrought let others weigh and measure.
> But thou sometimes wilt not forget,

When evening creeps across the pane,
The scent of shy blue violet
That sweetened all the plain.

Cordt was standing behind her chair when the song was finished. She did not perceive it, but sat with her hands on the keys and softly repeated the last lines.

He looked at her hair and her hands and at the white dress that hung over her shoulders and her lap. He knew as he had never known before what he had lost and knew that he would never win it back. His hands trembled, his eyes burned. He thought that he must kill her and himself.

Then he spoke her name.

She looked up and looked at him.

She forgot everything, saw nothing but him. He could see it in her great, strange eyes and in her red mouth.

And she sprang up with a cry of happiness and he took her in his arms and carried her away.

CHAPTER XI

The candles on the mantelpiece were lighted and their gleam fell through the balcony-door over the square, as it had done every evening since the house was built.

Outside, the square shone with a thousand lights. There was a sound of carriages, but at a distance, for the house was thrust a long way back and its walls were as thick as the walls of a castle.

And, when time passed and night came, the noise died away and you could hear the rippling of the fountain, which never begins and never stops, and cries, no one knowing what they are, solitary steps that approach and retreat again.

Cordt stood by the fireplace of the empty room.

He stared at the places where the quaint old things had stood which had seen his race pass through the room.

He remembered every single piece that had been brought there and looked at the empty spot where each had stood. He closed his eyes and saw everything in its place again ... the spinet sang ... Fru Adelheid's white train rustled over the carpet.

He thought of the man who had built the house and the room and who had called it the soul of the house and its tradition and its secret chamber. Of all those after him who had brought their wives in here ... of the day when he himself stood in the room for the first time.

And he went and opened the secret recess in the wall which hid the old, yellow document on which each of them who took possession of the room had written his name and his wife's.

He read the report of the builder of the house, with its plain, homely phrases.

And, when he had read it and read it again, he struck out his own name and Fru Adelheid's and went away and left the door open behind him.

PART II
CORDT'S SON

CHAPTER XII

WHEN Cordt had finished telling the story of the old room, he sat by the window and looked across the square, where the dusk was gathering about the newly-lighted lamps.

The servant entered noiselessly and lit the chandelier and went out noiselessly again. And the light filled the whole of the room and fell upon Cordt, who sat and gazed before him, and upon Finn, who stood by him with his eyes fixed on his face.

But Finn and Cordt were not where the light found them.

They were in the wonderful mystery of the old room. They heard the rippling of the fountain outside in the silent square; they saw the blaze of the red flowers on the balcony. The slender notes of the spinet sounded in their ears; Fru Adelheid's white gown rustled over the floor.

And, when Cordt turned his face towards his son, he appeared to Finn as a very big, old man; and Finn seemed to Cordt the little child that once lay and laughed in the cradle and fought with its little fat fists.

Then Cordt stood up and took Finn's arm and they walked to and fro, silent, overcome with what they had seen and afraid lest they should shatter the dream by speaking.

They walked for some time. And, when, at length, they stopped before the window, which was dewed with the heat, so that they could see nothing through it, Cordt remembered that there was still something which Finn ought to know and which he could not ask about.

He looked at Finn and remembered how he had loved his mother.

It was her eyes, but more restful-looking; her mouth, but paler and tired, as though it had tried a thousand times to say something which it never could. He had her slender waist and he was taller than Cordt, but carried his height like a burden. Then he also had Fru Adelheid's pale cheeks and forehead, but Cordt's hair, only thicker still and blacker.

"Finn," said Cordt and laid his hands on his shoulders.

Finn started and could not look at him. But Cordt took him under the chin and lifted his head and looked with a sad smile into his frightened eyes:

"There is only one thing left to tell you, Finn.... Fru Adelheid did not take a lover."

His smile widened when he saw his son's sudden and great joy; and he drew him to him and kissed him.

But then he suddenly left him and sat down somewhere in the room, with his back to him. Finn followed him and stood by him for a while and thought kindly and fondly of him and could find nothing to say.

The thoughts rushed through Cordt's head.

Now that he had lived through it all anew, the scab broke which the silence of many years had placed upon the wound in his will. His eyes grew hard and angry, he wanted to speak as he used to speak when he fought his hopeless fight for Fru Adelheid.

But then his glance fell upon Finn.

He sat as he liked best to sit, with bent head and his hands open upon his knees.

And Cordt grew gentle again and said, softly:

"You are glad, of course. For, you see, she is your mother."

He crossed the room and came back and stood with his arm over the back of the chair and looked at Finn, who was lost in his thoughts. It was silent in the room and silent outside, for it was Sunday. They could hear the bells ringing for evening service.

"She never secured the red flowers in the place of the blue which she valued so little," said Cordt, "I don't know ... I often thought...."

The bells rang out.

There was one that was quite close and one that was farther away, but louder, nevertheless. And there was a sound of distant bells which could not be distinguished from one another, but which sang in the air.

It sounded louder than it was, because they were thinking of it; and the ringing grew and filled the room with its deafening clamor.

Then there came a rumbling in the gateway. The carriage drove out in the soft snow, where they could not hear it.

"That's Fru Adelheid going to church," said Cordt.

He sat down by his son and began to talk in a low voice and without looking at him.

The bells rang and then suddenly stopped and increased the silence a hundredfold.

"There was a night at Landeck when the bells caught her, a night following upon a day of sunshine and merriment and many people. She was the gayest of us all and, in the evening, all at once, she became silent and tired, as so often happened, without any cause that I knew of.... You were with us. You were ten years old then; you lay and slept. We had been standing together by your bed and looking at you and she began to cry and I could do nothing but hold her hand in mine and stop speaking."

Finn listened, as he had just listened to the bells, without making out what the words had to tell him. He only knew that his mother was without blame and that his father had been able to tell it him all on that day and to leave it to him to pronounce judgment between himself and her. His joy at this sang within him and made all the rest easy and light and indifferent.

And Cordt continued:

"Then I went out on the verandah with my cigar and she stood in the doorway and listened to the bell of a little chapel up in the mountains, where we had been during the day. We had heard the story when we were there. Once, in the old days, a pious man had built the chapel in expiation of a sin and, since then, the bell had rung two hours after midnight every day.... She asked whether it would go on ringing till the end of the world and we came to talk of all the bells that ring over the earth, by day and by night, sun up and sun down, and comfort weary mortals.... Sometimes she was silent. But the bell rang up there constantly. And she constantly began to talk again and constantly about the same thing. About the bells that sounded so eternally and so identically over the whole world ... about those who heard them for the first time, one day when they were running like wild heathens in the endless wood ... about those whose will suddenly broke in the midst of the modern crowd, so that they fell on their knees and crept away where the bells summoned them."

Finn looked up. The words now caught his mind and he woke from his dreams.

"I see her before me still, as she stood on the night when she carried her soul to God. Her strange eyes lifted to the stars ... her white face ... her hands ... and her words, which came so quickly, as though her life depended upon their coming, and so heavily, as though every one of them caused her pain. She never gave it a thought that I was there: she spoke as though she were doing public penance in the church-porch.... And then she declared that it was over.... It had become empty around her and cold and dark to anguish and despair, there where her glad eyes had beamed upon the lights and the crowd of the feast. Despair had come long since and slowly and she had closed her eyes to it and denied it. It had grown and come nearer to her and she had run away from it, as though she were running for her life. Now it was there and reached from earth to heaven, in her, around her, far and wide. And, if the bells could not conquer it, then she must die."

Cordt spoke so softly that Finn could hardly catch his words.

"Then the bell up there ceased. Soon after, the day dawned and the sun shone on her white, moist cheeks. She was still now and silent, but her thoughts were the same. When things began to stir around us, in the town and at the hotel, she went out, I did not know where, but I daresay she was at the chapel. Towards evening, she returned and, at midnight, we sat on the verandah again and listened to the church-bell.... A week passed thus. I often feared for her reason. She always talked of the same thing and it was almost worse when she was silent. I sent old Hans home with you and, the next day, we left. But it was long before we reached home. She wanted to travel by the same road which we had taken on the journey out. She said she wanted to pray in every church which she had passed on her hunt for happiness through the world."

Finn half raised himself in his chair:

"And did you?" he asked.

"I did as she wished. It became a pilgrimage to every region where life lies nakedest in its pleasure. Restlessly we travelled from place to place. She omitted none, afraid lest there should remain a single sin which she had not prayed away, a single memory which the bells had not rung into the grave."

"And then did you come home?"

Cordt looked at his son as if he had forgotten that he was in the room. He suddenly awoke to the consciousness of what lay between those days and these; and his face became so gloomy and his eyes so serious that Finn was frightened.

"Then we came home. And then...."

He rose quickly and stood with his arms crossed on his breast and looked at Finn:

"Then we came home. And the years passed and Fru Adelheid recovered her peace of mind. She found herself again and became the same as in the old days. Her thoughts waver restlessly, her desires yearn insatiably. Her carriage now rattles through the streets as before ... only it stops at the church instead of the theatre."

Finn wanted to speak, but could not, because Cordt stood in front of him and looked at him fixedly and nodded to him, once, as if to say that he knew what it was and that it was no use.

"She goes to Heaven's table," said Cordt, "and Heaven comes to her parties."

Finn sank back in his chair.

He was surprised and ashamed that he was not grieved with his father for saying that, nor with his mother, if it were true. He knew that he ought to rouse himself to protest or sympathy, but could not, because he understood it all so well.

But Cordt crossed the room with a firm stride:

"Heaven is not what Fru Adelheid thinks, nor where she seeks it," he said. "Perhaps you will not understand me until you have lived longer in the world; but look here, Finn ... what I have seen of God in my life I have seen most in those who denied Him. In their sense of responsibility, in their humanity ... in their pride I have seen God's splendor. The others, those who confess His name and fill His house ... they masked Him from me so closely, when they ought to glorify Him, made Him so small, when they praised His might...."

He talked about this for a time. Finn sat dumb and helpless in his chair and wished his father would cease. He felt like one who has inadvertently witnessed something he ought not to see, or like one who is receiving a confidence under a false pretence.

And deep down within him lay a little ironical astonishment at the fire and authority with which his father was talking.

But, at that moment, Cordt sat down in front of him with both his hands in his own and sad and gentle eyes and words as soft and humble as though he were a sinner begging for peace:

"I don't know, Finn. I cannot really tell you anything about it. I can never talk with you about these things. A father is a poor creature, Finn, and I am a poor father. I cannot tell you that the forest is green and that the birds sing and that there is nothing behind the blue sky. I dare not, Finn. I do not think I have the right to. I cannot go to church with you, either ... nor even be glad when you go with your mother."

He pressed Finn's hands nervously. They lay dead in his and Finn did not know what to do with his eyes.

"But I must talk to you a little ... just this once ... to-day, when I have confessed to you and made up your parents' accounts. If you will try to understand me ... and to forgive me ... to forgive us, because we are not so rich as our child could expect ... since we have a child.... You love the bells, Finn. When they ring, you fall a-dreaming; they ring you far away from where you are. You were like that ever since you were a little boy. And I can well understand it. I love them, too. I am glad because they are there. But ... Finn ... Finn, there are so many bells in the world besides those which summon us to church. Every man has his own, which are his and his only ... which he alone can hear, which call no one but him. There are men, opulent, charming men, for whom the bells ring wherever they set foot. They lead more powerful lives than we and prouder lives. They suffer us ... those of us who love them. But there is not in the world a man so small but that the bells call him. One has them in his work, Finn. And one in his child ... and one in his love. For one they hang in a neat little room where his mother lives and where he can only come for an hour, perhaps ... on a Sunday.... It is not the same for the one as for the other, Finn, but the bells are there always. They call their man back when he has strayed from the way he should go, or, if that is too late, they ring for his remorse. They ring to the banquet and they ring their music when he is tired and sad.... But the church-bells ... they ring for the man whose ears life has deafened ... and life makes such a terrible noise. They ring on Sundays to remind us of that which we have forgotten throughout the week.... And it is well that they are there.... But ... Finn ... it is so tragic when the church-bells drive and tumble people together who once had each his own sacred church. It is just as when a home breaks up and the old find a refuge in the workhouse. The sun shines through the windows and it is warm indoors and there are flowers in the casement. But there was once something that was better.... For your mother and me, Finn ... for us the bells used to ring in the old room."

He was silent and no longer looked at Finn. And Finn was at ease again and at last found words for what he had long wanted to say:

"May I use the old room, father? May I set it up again ... all as it was ... and live there with my books?..."

Cordt released his son's hands and his face wore a look that made Finn regret his request. They both rose to their feet. And, at that moment, Cordt's face lit up with a smile:

"That you may," he said. "You dear child, who never asked for anything. Let this, then, be my present to you to-day."

This happened on the day when Cordt's son completed his twenty-first year.

CHAPTER XIII

Finn stood in the old room with the yellow document in his hand:

> "God brought me thus far, that I was able to erect this fair house, which shall stand till distant times, a witness to my might and that of my race. Here shall be upright living and generous dealing; the house shall be faithfully guarded from father to son; good men and women shall sit in the hall and dance to the sound of flutes and violins.
>
> "I have placed this room in the most secret part of the house and no one knows of it but the architect who built it and my oldest servant. But I have sealed the architect's tongue with a solemn oath and a heavy fee; and my servant is true to me.
>
> "I have decorated the room with gilt and figured leather hangings and costly carpets from the East. I have had two great armchairs made in Milan, whose woodwork is carved into birds and animals which grin strangely in the dark, but cease to do so when the lights are lit.
>
> "Then I gave my servant a key of the room and told him to care for it faithfully. Every evening, when it grows dusk, he is to light the candles on the mantelpiece; and he is to do this even if he know that his master is travelling in distant lands. Every morning, he is to adjust the room with his own hands. None but himself is ever to cross the threshold.
>
> "For this room shall be for me and my wife and for none other in the world. Therefore I placed it in the most secluded part of the house, far from the counting-house, where we work, from the passages, along which our servants go, and from the drawing-room, where we receive our guests, ay, even from our marriage-bed, where she sleeps by my side.

> "It shall be the temple of our marriage, hallowed by our love, which is greater than anything that we know. Here we will pray to Him Who gave us to each other. Here we will talk gladly and earnestly, every evening when our hearts impel us to. And, when we come to die, our son shall bring his wife here and they shall do as we did.
>
> "This evening, which is the first in my new house, I brought my wife in here and told her my wish. She listened to my words in love and gladness and I have written down in this document how it all happened and we have set our names to it in witness for those who come after us."

Finn read their names and the names of those who had taken possession of the room after the builder and his wife. Last of all stood Cordt's name and Fru Adelheid's, which were struck out again.

Then he put the document back in its place and locked it up and looked round the room.

The old room stood again as it used to stand, built high over the square, long and deep and silent, like a spot where there is no life.

The balcony was white with snow and the sparrows hopped in the snow. Inside, behind the colored panes, stood many red flowers and longed for the sun. The dust had been removed from the figured-leather hangings, which shone with a new brightness. The oriental carpet spread over the floor like a lord returning from exile and once more taking possession of his estates.

And all the old glories had found their places again and stood as lawfully and restfully as though it had never been otherwise. The spinet was there and the jar with the man writhing through thorns and the celestial globe whose stars shone and ran: all the furniture which the room's different owners had set there in the course of time, each after his own taste and heart.

Before the fireplace stood the two great, strange armchairs.

Finn felt as if he were in a cathedral where every flag was a tombstone over a famous man. His senses drank the odor of the bygone times, his fancy peopled the room with the men and women who had sat there and exchanged strong and gentle words, while the house lay sleeping around them.

With it all, he became lost in thought of those who had sat there last and after whom no others were to come, those two who had given him the life which he knew not what to do with.

He saw them before him in the love and struggle of their youth. He heard their voices in the room, he saw Fru Adelheid's red mouth and Cordt's steady eyes. He saw Cordt bring his wife into the room, which was the soul of the house and its tradition and its secret chamber, and show her the strange things which his ancestors had put there.

He saw him on the day when he stood alone by the fireplace ... in the empty room ... and struck out his own name and Fru Adelheid's from the document and went away and left the door open behind him....

He saw all this as it had happened. But they were not his father and mother. They were two attractive people of whom he had read in a book and grown fond, as a man loves art, palely and with no self-seeking in his desire.

Finn drew one of the big chairs over to the window and sat down and sat there for long.

He was sitting there when Fru Adelheid came.

She stood in the doorway, in her white gown, with her white hair, and nodded to him. Then she turned her face round to the room and looked at it.

And then that happened which was only the shadow of a dream that vanished then and there: everything came to life in the room.

The spinet sang, the queer faces on the old chairs raised themselves on their long necks; there was a whispering and a muttering in every corner....

Fru Adelheid shrank back against the door. She did not see Finn, did not remember that he was there.

But Finn saw her.

He rose from his chair and his eyes beamed:

"You light up the room, mother," he said, "and the room lights up you."

He took her hand and kissed it and, with her hand in his, Fru Adelheid went through the old room, which had been too narrow for her youthful desires.

The fairy-tale was over and the dread. But the glow still lay over her figure and made her look wonderfully pretty. Her cheeks were as pink as a girl's; her step was light, her eyes moist and shy. She laughed softly and gladly, while she looked at the old things and talked about them and touched them.

She told the story of the woman who used to sing when she was sad and who had brought the old spinet there; and her hands shook as she struck a chord and the slender, beautiful notes sounded through the room.

Of the spinning-wheel, which had whirred merrily every evening for many a good year and which stood as it was, with thread upon the spindle. Of the celestial globe, which had been the toy of the man whose intellect was obscured. Of the doll with the vacant face, which stood there in memory of the lady who dreaded the deep silence of the room and never entered it but once; but her son, who loved her, had hidden the doll in the curtain. Of Fru Lykke, whose portrait had hung where the light stain was, but hung there no longer, because her marriage had been dissolved.

Of the jar with the man writhing through thorns, which she herself had brought as her gift, she said nothing. She passed her hand over its bright surface and was silent.

Finn's eyes clung to her.

Never had he seen his beautiful mother so beautiful. He did not know that look, or that smile on her mouth, or that clear ring in her voice.

At times, he added something to what she was telling and spoke with such profound intelligence that she was quite surprised and frightened. Now he guessed her words before she uttered them. Then he knew something which she had never suspected.

Secretly, her fear increased as to what Cordt could have told him.

But Finn was lost in his delight.

And, fascinated by her beauty and the strange things he had seen and heard and the deep silence of the room, he forgot that the seal of the old room was broken and wished to play the game as vividly as possible.

He drew the second of the two big chairs across to the window and made her sit down and sat himself beside her:

"Now you are not my mother," he said. "You are my young bride. I have brought you into the sanctuary to-day and now I will initiate you into the mysteries."

Fru Adelheid turned very pale and Finn took her hand penitently:

"Have I hurt you, mother?"

She shook her head and forced herself to smile.

Then he walked into the room again and rejoiced at all this and talked about it. But she remained sitting with knitted brow.

She was heavy at heart, because it seemed to her, all at once, that she was not his mother, as they sat talking here in the secret chamber of the house. The old days came in their great might; and their strong memories and impressive words drowned the bells which had rung her into another world.

It was the echo here, in the old room, of Cordt's words and of his love ... of the strong faith and great happiness of the race which had sprouted in the good mould of tradition and produced flower after flower in the times that passed.

Fru Adelheid thought—for a moment—that it would have been well had things happened as Cordt wished.

But, at the same instant, she was seized by a thought that suddenly made her rebellious and young, as when she was here last, many years ago.

She thrust her chair back hard and looked with sparkling eyes round the room where everything and every memory was hostile to her.

She looked at Finn, who was standing by the celestial globe and trying to set it going, but could not, because the spring was rusty and refused to work.

She wondered, when the time came for Finn to take a wife ... would he try to revive the tradition and bring her here and sit down with her in the old chairs?

Then Finn's son and his son after him would read her name, which was written on the yellow document and struck out again. She would be like one of those who were branded in that family.... Legends would grow about her love of going out and her hunt after happiness which did not exist....

"Come and help me, mother," said Finn.

She went over and pressed hard on the spring and the clockwork hummed.

"See how you let loose the magic," he said.

He went on talking, delighted with the stars, which lit up and ran.

"Sit down here by me, Finn."

She waited till he came and a little longer, as though she could not find the words she wanted, and did not look at him while she spoke:

"Finn" she said and put her hand on his shoulder and drew it away again immediately. "Finn ... once ... ever so many years ago, I was alone, one evening, in the old room. I had often been here before, you know ... with father. And I was under the power of the old room and never happy. I was young, Finn, and it went so terribly hard with my longing and my gladness. I could not understand that and could not mitigate it or get over it. For father belonged to the room and it was his and all the queer things in it and they were all against me. Every time I came to the door, my heart stopped beating.... And once I was inside ... it was ... it was as if my own words were taken from my tongue and others put in their place for me to speak ... beautiful words and good words, Finn, but not mine. But then, when I took courage and said what I wanted to say, it sounded as if I was defying the old room and father and God himself. And then...."

Fru Adelheid felt that she was on the point of betraying something great and fine that had been laid in her hands. She looked round as if she were afraid that there was some one in the room or that the room itself would rise up against her in its venerable might.

But there was no one and it was silent.

Then she turned her face to Finn and looked at him and said, gaily:

"But that evening, Finn, I broke the spell of the old room. I tore the veil from the Holy of Holies and saw that there was nothing behind it. For the first time, I breathed freely in my own home."

Fru Adelheid did not tell how, at the same moment, she had been overcome by terror and fled from the room. But she did not gain what she thought by her lie. For Finn looked at her sorrowfully and said:

"How could you do that, mother? How could you find it in your heart?"

"Are you also under the spell?" she asked.

There was in her tone a scorn which was stronger than she intended and which frightened herself. But Finn simply paid no attention to it:

"The old room no longer exists," he said. "It is nothing more than an image, a monument ... my fancy, which father humored me in."

She turned her face away and listened.

"But had I lived in the days of the old room," he said, "then it would certainly have captured me and held me captive."

"Yes ... you have been talking to father," she said, softly.

"Yes."

Then he lay down before her, with his cheek on her hand, as he so often did:

"Yes," he repeated. "And ... mother ... I love you. You are so pretty. But we will not talk about the old room ... ever. For I think it is the most wonderful ... and the most beautiful and the strongest thing I know of.... But it hurts me that I am not wholly your son ... or father's either, that I might devote myself to one of you in sharing your strongest feelings. And I cannot talk to father about it ... neither can we two, can we?"

Fru Adelheid did not answer him, but stroked his hair with her hand. Neither of them spoke and it was quite silent in the room.

In the silence she became herself again. The many moulded years came to their own again and the bells rang monotonously and ever more strongly from out of the noise of the world, which had drowned them.

She marvelled at the excitement into which the old room had thrown her. Quenched was the love which had made her its mistress and quenched the red desire which made it too narrow. She thought of Cordt, who had fought, she considered, for what was not worth fighting for. Sorrowfully she looked at her tall, silent boy, whose weary thoughts kept pace so well with her own.

She crossed her hands in her lap and the light faded in her eyes. The glow of the old room withdrew from her face, her words became restful as her thoughts.

Finn looked at her, but did not see this. For him, too, the fairy-tale was over. He was sitting in his chair again with bent head and his hands open on his knees.

And, without their doing anything or thinking of it, they came in their usual way to talk together. It was not any interchange of thoughts and still less a contest of opinions. They said nearly the same thing and, wherever the thoughts of the one roamed, he found the other's. Often their words were solemn, but never powerful. Often the one was silent and agreed with the other. Many times they sat long without saying anything and thought they had told each other everything.

"Look," said Finn, pointing out of the window. "How hideous!"

A hearse came trotting across the square.

He moved in his chair and said:

"A hearse should always drive at a foot's pace, solemnly and ceremoniously ... always ... as though they were only driving the horses to water. And soldiers should always hold themselves stiff and starched, keeping step and time, even when they are taking their shoes to the cobbler's. Then it would all be easier."

He was silent for a while. Then he slowly turned his face to her:

"I was talking about it to father the other day," he said. "I happened to say something of the kind."

She looked at him in surprise.

"I don't know how it came about. But he laughed and said I ought to write an article about it or form a society for preserving the correct pace of hearses."

Fru Adelheid smiled and laid her hands in her lap and looked at them.

"Then he suddenly became serious and came up to me and laid his hands on my shoulders: 'Hearses ought to drive fast,' he said, 'gallop ... at a rousing pace. Away with the dead, Finn! Let life grow green and blossom!'"

"Father is so masterful," said Fru Adelheid.

Finn nodded.

Then they began to talk about Cordt. They often did so. And they were always eager to find good words to praise him in. But under the words there lay the consciousness, like a secret understanding between them, that he was made of a coarser clay than they.

They never said this; but they felt a sort of patronizing pity for him, such as one feels for a person who runs and runs, when it is good to sit still.

But, when they talked together, Fru Adelheid knew that deep in Finn's soul there lay a secret yearning towards just that masterful side in his father which frightened him.

It was so weak, only a pale reflection of her own young love, a distant echo of the voice which had stated Cordt's case in her own heart when he was fighting to win her.

But it was enough to hurt her. She thought she only had her son for a time. She traced a certain disdain in the intimacy to which he admitted her. She thought there was something in him which was greater than what he gave her and which was Cordt's or would become so.

And she realized that the fight for Finn would become harder than that which broke the seal on the door of the old room.

Finn was absorbed in what had filled his mind, the whole day, with light and color. He was thinking now of his mother's visit to the room on the evening when she had broken the spell:

"I simply cannot understand how you could have the heart," he said.

She knew at once what he meant, but said nothing.

"There ought to be some law, like that in the fairy-story, where he who lifted the veil had to die," he said. "And there ought to be veils upon veils ...

veils upon veils.... Can you bear to look at the sun, mother? Women ought to go in a veil and never ... never raise it, except when the occasion was so great that everything grew great.... And one ought not to see the people who play...."

Fru Adelheid half raised herself in her chair.

She wanted to tell him that, on that evening, she was punished for her presumption with the greatest terror which she had ever experienced in her life. But she could not. Then she said, quite quietly and with her eyes looking out over the square:

"And suppose there were some one who could not ... suppose the veil stifled one...."

Finn looked out into space like her:

"Veils upon veils.... Veils over the dead," he said.

Fru Adelheid sighed and said nothing.

"Then one could live," said Finn.

CHAPTER XIV

From that day onward, Finn only left the old room when obliged.

The spring had opened the fountain before the house and he was happy at its rippling, which never began and never stopped. The red flowers were put out on the balcony: when the wind blew, their petals fluttered right over into the basin of the fountain and rocked upon the water. He followed their dance through the air and wondered if they would reach their goal.

His best time was in the evening, when the square shone with a thousand lights.

He loved the dying day.

He knew every light that went out, every sound as it stopped. And he liked the sound best when it stopped and the light when it went out. He thought that the people who moved down below, disguised in the darkness, were of another kind or better than those whom the sun shone upon. He had no more to do with them than with the others; but he liked them better.

Then, when night came and the rippling of the fountain sang louder and louder through the silence and cries sounded from down below, no one knowing what they were, and solitary steps were heard, that approached and retreated again, then he lit the candles on the mantelpiece and sat down in one of the old chairs, there where the owners of the house and their wives had sat when the house slept and they had something to say to each other.

He looked round the room, where the things sang in every dark corner, and simply could not conceive that he had not known the old room before.

He was more at home here than anywhere else: here, where he was outside the world, which worried him, because it demanded that of him which he had not; here, where every spot and every object told how all had been said and done and accomplished in the old days, so that he had nothing else to do but listen wonderingly and rejoice at its marvellous beauty.

Then he fell a-dreaming and remained sitting till the lights went out.

"He does not sleep enough," said Fru Adelheid, anxiously.

Cordt crossed the floor with the same thought in his mind. Then he stopped where she was sitting and looked at her:

"I wonder, is he ever awake, Adelheid?" he said.

By day, Finn generally sat at the window and stared out, idly and silently, with his hands open on his knees.

Often, when Cordt was crossing the square, he thought that he could see Finn's old face behind the window-panes. He would stop and nod and beckon to him.

But Finn never saw him. For he saw nothing positively.

And Cordt went on ... in and out ... constantly longing to see the strong air of the old room color his son's cheeks and rouse his will ... constantly trusting that, sooner or later, this would happen.

He never went up there since the day when he and his old servant had arranged the room as it used to be.

And Finn was glad of this. He was so afraid lest that should happen that a long time passed before he could suppress his terror when he heard any one coming. And, even when he had recovered his composure, he knew that it would happen sooner or later and that the day of its happening would be a gloomy one.

For he well understood the eternal loving question in Cordt's eyes and it hurt him and frightened him. He dreaded the craving in his affection, which was greater than a father's. It was like that of a sovereign for the heir who is to occupy the throne after him.

And Finn could not take the reins of empire in his slack hands or bear the pressure of the crown upon his head, which ached at the mere thought of it.

But Fru Adelheid often came; and they two were comfortable up there, in the old room.

She came with no craving; and, if she was doubtful and restless, as she often was since Finn had moved up into the old room, then she would be quite silent when the door closed behind her.

Silent like Finn ... and like the big chairs and the jar with the man writhing through thorns ... silent like the spinning-wheel, which had whirred merrily every evening for many a good year and stood as it was with thread upon its spindle.

He looked at her and smiled and nodded when she spoke. He himself talked ... for long at a time and then stopped, without its making any difference, and listened to the rippling of the fountain and the voices in the old room, which always talked to him and plainest when Fru Adelheid was with him.

He told her that, when she came, the room was no longer his own.

For then he felt like a stranger, a man of another period, who should suddenly find himself in an old ruined castle, full of marvellous dangers and adventures, and stand face to face with the last of those who had lived the castle's rich, wonderful life.

Once he spoke her name aloud just as she was entering at the door. It was dark in the room and his voice and figure were so like Cordt's that she grew pale and frightened. But he did not see this and she forced a laugh and soon forgot it.

And, gradually, the wonderful solemnity of the old room retreated into the background, when they were both there, for they spent more and more of their time there and at last simply did not think they were together except there. But Finn was always able to summon it up when he wished.

They used to read together.

And that happened in this way, that one of them found a book, a treasure of silence and singing, which was the only sort that they felt equal to, and read it and gave it to the other, who then read it while they were together.

They found most of the books in foreign languages and it seemed as if there were no end of them. Also, the fact that the language was foreign made the book dearer to them, because it carried them farther afield.

When they had read one of these books, they lived in it for a time ... not in its action, among its characters, for there was no action and no characters, but in its music. They tuned their thoughts and words in its key.

Then they felt as if they had passed through some experience or as if they were travelling.

"The artist lives," said Finn. "He makes the sky blue and grey for himself ... for himself and for us all. He wipes everything out with his hand and builds it up again ... greater, ever greater. He is the master. He is God."

One day, he asked Fru Adelheid to sing.

She had not sung for many years, except in church, and was surprised at his request:

"I have given up singing, Finn."

He lay down before her and looked up smiling into her face:

"I can remember so well when you used to sing," he said. "You often sang to me when I was a boy. But one occasion ... one occasion I remember in particular. There were many visitors and I, of course, had long been in bed, but I was not asleep. For old Marie had promised to take me down to the dining-room when the people had got up from dinner and you were to sing. She told me that, when there was company and all the candles were lighted and you were prettiest and brightest, then you sang a thousand times more beautifully than usual."

She took her eyes from his face and laid her head back in her chair.

"I kept awake till she came and it lasted long. But then I heard you and also saw you for a moment through the door."

"And was it so nice?"

"I don't remember," he said. "But I remember the many faces.... I should know them again if I saw them now, I think. And best of all I remember father's."

Fru Adelheid rose:

"What shall I sing?" she asked.

He laughed with content, went to the spinet and opened it. Then he took up one of the pieces of music:

"Look what I have found," he said. "This was sung by the one who put the spinet here. Look, here is her name: she herself wrote both the words and the music.... See how pale the writing is ... and how distinct."

Fru Adelheid stood with the old, yellow sheet in her hand. She hummed the tune and struck the keys.

Then she sat down to the spinet and sang:

> Day is passing, dearest maiden:
> Ere thou knowest, comes the night;
> Warning winds, with fragrance laden,
> Bring cool air and colder light.
> We must part: time hastens so!
> Day is passing, dew is falling.
> Hark! Thy mother's voice is calling:
> Dearest maiden, I must go.
>
> Part we must, dear maid, in sorrow!
> Day is surely doomed to die.
> Ah, but we shall find to-morrow
> Countless joys we let go by,
> Countless words we uttered not,

Hours we robbed of wasted chances,
Eyes we balked of mutual glances,
Countless kisses we forgot.

Happy smiles will haunt thee dreaming
On a couch of virgin white;
In my brain thy picture gleaming,
I shall hasten through the night.
Let the crimson sun depart!
Brighter sunshine in thy face is,
Sunshine of remembered places,
Love's own sunshine in thy heart.

She remained sitting a while with the old music-sheet in her hand. Then Finn said:

"She used to sing that. Do you know if she was happy, mother?"

"She was often sad," said Fru Adelheid. "And, when she was sad, she sang."

She put down the sheet and took up the first music-book that came to hand, but threw it aside, as though it had burnt her fingers.

It was the Lenore songs, which she had sung to Cordt.

She rose and went back to her place beside Finn. Then she sprang up and stood with her arms crossed on her breast and sat down again and stared with great eyes through the window:

"Finn ... if I sang it to you ... would you recognize the ... the song you heard when Marie carried you down...?"

He woke from his dream and looked at her in surprise:

"The song ... no ... I should not. Why, do you remember it?"

"No," said Fru Adelheid.

They long sat silent. Twilight fell and it grew dark in the room.

"Mother," said Finn, "what are women like?"

She turned her face slowly towards him. He did not look at her. His eyes were far away and she realized that he had forgotten his question or did not know that he had put it.

CHAPTER XV

Fru Adelheid stood in her wraps at the window and looked out. The horses were stamping in the porch below; the footman stood by the carriage-door and waited.

They were going to the station to fetch Finn.

He had been abroad the whole summer.

This was the first time he had been away alone and he had not enjoyed himself abroad. From Florence, Spain and Paris he had written to ask if he might not come home. But Cordt was resolved that he should remain abroad for the time agreed upon.

He wrote oftenest to Fru Adelheid ... and stupidly and awkwardly, because he knew that his father would read the letters. Cordt noticed this, but said nothing. He hurried through the letters as though he were looking for something positive and put them down with a face as though he had not found it.

He always gave Fru Adelheid the letters he received, although she never asked for them.

Fru Adelheid looked impatiently at her watch. She sat down, closed her eyes and pressed her forehead against the pane.

She thought how empty the house had been during the summer.

Cordt had not said a word about the old room, but, from the day when Finn had moved up there, things had altered between him and her. Something had happened ... something indefinite and nameless, but none the less fateful on that account.

And, while Finn was abroad, this had grown between them ... without their doing anything to further or prevent it. Neither of them thought about it. Both led their own lives and drifted farther apart in their yearning for their quiet child. The day was long for them, their rooms were cold.

But inside her was a growing anxiety for Cordt, who became ever more silent and wore such a melancholy look in his eyes.

A door opened and she sprang up:

"We shall be late, Cordt."

"Not at all," he said, calmly. "You ordered the carriage too early."

"Let us go, Cordt. We may just as well wait there as here."

Cordt sat down with his hat on his knee and looked at her. She stood with bent head and buttoned her gloves.

"Sit down for a moment," he said and pushed a chair towards her.

"Do you want to talk to me?"

"Sit down, Adelheid," he said, impatiently. "Sit down for a moment."

Fru Adelheid leant against the chair and remained standing.

"It is long since we talked together, Adelheid ... many, many years. Do you know that?"

She shrugged her shoulders:

"Very likely," she said and made her voice as firm as she could. "We have peace now, you see."

Cordt nodded. He drummed with his fingers on his hat and looked out of the window:

"Yes ... yes, no doubt. We are old, Adelheid. As old as can be."

"Is that what you wanted to say to me?"

"I am afraid for Finn," said Cordt. "He will come home as pale as when he went away, a poor dreamer by the grace of God. To-morrow, he will be sitting up there and staring out at the life he dare not live."

"Yes ... why should he be up in the old room?"

"It was he who asked me," said Cordt, calmly. "I could not deny him his inheritance. He has the right to know the ground he sprang from."

"And what then? Do you think you can bring the dead days to life again?"

"No," he said. "I don't think that. I don't want that."

He was silent for a little. She did not take her eyes from his face. Then he said:

"Finn can build himself a new house, if he likes. Or he can refurnish his ancestral halls. And put in plate-glass windows and wide staircases and anything that suits him and his period. But he must know and be thankful that the walls are strong and the towers tall."

Fru Adelheid pushed back the chair she was leaning against:

"There does not appear to be room for a mother in your arrangement," she said.

Her voice trembled, her eyes were large and angry. But Cordt rose and looked as calm as before:

"You went out of it, Adelheid. You did not wish to be there."

She made no reply. She understood that he did not mean to consult her, to ask her for her help ... did not even want it.

"Adelheid ... now that Finn is coming...."

"Yes?..."

"I am afraid for him, Adelheid. And I would ask you to be on your guard and do him no harm. I believe that sometimes you smother his poor, dejected spirit. The peace which you have gained may be good in itself and good for you ... but he is young, you must remember. He is only at the start of life, he has no need for peace and resignation. What is a boon to you is death to him, perhaps...."

She took a step forward and raised her face close up to his:

"Now it has come to this, Cordt, that you think I am your enemy for Finn's sake."

"You may become so," he said.

"You will drive me to it, Cordt."

He took her hand and held it tight when she tried to draw it away:

"No," he said. "No, Adelheid. I only want to warn you."

CHAPTER XVI

The balcony-door was standing open, because they had forgotten to close it. But the weather was mild and there was hardly any wind. Now and again, a yellow leaf fell somewhere or other from the baluster. It began to grow dusk.

Fru Adelheid sat with her head in her hands and stared out before her.

Cordt's words kept ringing in her ears. She did not think either that Finn was as he used to be. He was restless, could not sit still, talked more than usual:

"Wherever I went, I found the fountain outside," he said. "It followed me throughout my journey. There was not a rushing noise so strong but the fountain sounded through it nor a night so still but it came rippling and sang me home again to the old room.... I wonder, did one of the owners of this house set it up?" he asked.

"I don't think so."

"Yes," said Finn. "That must be it. I am sure of it. Perhaps it was the one who built the house. You see, it forms part and parcel of the old room ... it sums it all up. If there was nothing else but the fountain, it would all be here just the same. I must ask father."

She shivered with cold and Finn shut the door:

"We are chilly people," he said. "Both of us. We are not like father. He laughed at me yesterday when I came down to his room to say good-morning and wanted to shut the window. 'Don't, Finn,' he said. 'The autumn air is bracing and healthy, it makes one young again ... sit in the draught and don't be afraid, old man that you are!'"

"Yes, father is strong."

Finn looked at her stealthily.

He had soon understood that his parents had drifted apart while he was abroad; and he suffered in consequence. He was as kind and affectionate to his mother as ever; but his thoughts were always harking back to Cordt, whatever they might be talking of:

"Father is so sad," he said.

"I haven't noticed it."

She colored after saying this. But Finn was not looking at her, scarcely heard her reply:

"It was strange, mother ... out there, on my journey, ever so many times I had a feeling that I came upon father. Wherever I went, I would suddenly hear his voice ... then he would be close to me, I walked with him, regulated my step by his and talked to him."

He laid his head back in his chair and closed his eyes:

"Often it was as if he had been where I came and prepared everything for me, so that I saw him in every corner. Sometimes I felt that I must put off my departure until he came."

"And did he come?"

"Always. Wasn't that strange?"

"Yes."

Fru Adelheid thought the sound of his voice was different from ordinary. He did not look at her, as he was used to do ... his thoughts were not with her.

"Where were you and father to-day?" she asked.

"We went out into the woods ... a long way out. Father was silent, but not so bored as at home. It was so lovely out there ... and so strange. One could hardly see a thing ... for the leaves falling."

"Yes," said Fru Adelheid.

Then she bent over him to look into his face, which had grown thinner and paler during the time that he was away:

"Finn," she said, "was I not with you ... out there ... when you were travelling?"

Finn smiled and nodded his head:

"You came in your letters," he said. "That father never did. But you were mostly here at home, where I was longing to be."

She thought it was strange that he did not take her hand when he said that.

And, suddenly, she became conscious that she was sitting in terror lest he should slip away from her.

What had she to hold him with, if anything seized him that was stronger than their quiet life in these hours ... what had she, if he went...?

It seemed to her as though Cordt stood in the room and beckoned him out into the yellow woods, where the air was so bracing and good. And Finn leapt up with a joyful cry ... they went away ... and never looked back....

She felt that Cordt was stronger than she and hated him for it. She sought for a weapon to defend herself. She wished that Finn, who loved her, would lie down before her, as he so often used to do, with his cheek against her hand. And she knew that he was not thinking of it.

She felt so wretched and so lonely that she grew frightened and called upon her old longing for the red happiness ... if only it would come and take her, so that she might have something to set against him who had everything....

"Sing to me, mother," said Finn.

"Yes," she said.

She crossed the room with a stronger step than usual. Her cheek was red and her eyes glowed. She took hold of the instrument with firm hands when she opened it. Finn noticed this and looked at her in surprise; but it was not light enough for him to make out her face.

Lovs't thou the peasant in his cosy cottage-nook?
Thou shalt share bed and board with him, eating and sleeping;
Thou shalt tranquilly brew and merrily cook;
Dusty wheel, rusty needle thy care shall not brook;
Thou shalt bless sun and rain in God's keeping.
But she that loves none shall go weeping!

Lovs't thou the poet with harp all of gold?
Thou shalt list to his song o'er the loud strings sweeping;
Thou shalt meet him, where flowrets peep from the wold;
By thy smiles shall his going and coming be told,
His mind in thy joyfulness steeping.
But she that loves none shall go weeping!

Lovs't thou the lordling, who hunts in the grove?
Thou shalt sue to thy mother and fly from her keeping;
Thou shalt give him thy lips and give him thy love;
Thou shalt take, as he flings horse or hound from above,
Blows, fame and food flung to thee creeping.

But she that loves none shall go weeping!

Fru Adelheid remained sitting with bowed head.

The song had broken her pride. She trembled over all her body and great tears fell upon her hands. She had conjured up spirits which she could not lay; she felt more powerless and small than she had ever felt before.

She began to think of Finn and looked round in alarm. But he could not see her and she wept silently. She laid her forehead against the spinet ... then her hand fell upon the keyboard and she started and rose from her seat.

"That was a strange song," said Finn.

It was so still in the room that she could not bear it.

"I have not sung it for many years," she said. "In the old days, I used to sing it often."

"What was father like when you met him?" asked Finn.

She stood with her back to him and turned the pages of the music with trembling hands.

"Was he as handsome as now?"

"Yes ... no.... I don't know if he was handsome."

Finn listened.

"He was ... he was charming."

"That he was ... that he was," he said and clapped his hands like a child who is delighted with a story. "And then he was so masterful ... was he not?... So that one was bound to follow him?"

"Yes," said Fru Adelheid.

"Father was a king," said Finn.

Her heart throbbed, she listened with all her senses. She felt that Finn was somewhere close to her and accomplishing something that would destroy her. And she could not turn round, could not go to him and beg him to desist.

"I could wish I had a brother," said Finn.

"Do you feel lonely?"

"No ... no, it is not that. But then he should have the kingdom."

CHAPTER XVII

At that time, Finn made a friend whom he had not chosen or wanted for himself, but whom Cordt gave him in his anxiety, because he thought he could never get any one better.

His name was Hans and they had known each other since they were children. He was a year older than Finn, not quite so tall, but more powerfully developed, with bright hair and eyes and disposition.

His father was a little man who sat among the people in the counting-house, where his father had sat before him. He and his little wife had no luck in life save their son. But at times they trembled for his future, because his ideas were so pronounced and took so wide a range.

For, even as he was taller than his father, so he would not be content with his measure in anything.

Above all, he did not want to sit in the office, but to go out in the world, big as it was. And, from the time when he was a little boy, he believed that it was bigger than they told him.

Now that he had grown up and become conscious of his need and his powers and could not get anywhere, he went fearlessly to the master of the house and told him how the matter stood.

Cordt liked him and wanted to keep him for his house, but soon saw that he had nothing that could tempt him. He asked him what he would like to be; and it appeared that Hans wanted to be an engineer.

Cordt looked at him and thought that his glance could blast rocks.

Then he promised his assistance and remained sitting in deep thought, while Hans went down the stairs singing.

Time passed. He advanced along his road and both he and the others could see that he was fully keeping pace with his dreams. Cordt did not lose sight of him and was pleased when he called. But Fru Adelheid did not like him, because he talked so loud and had such a heavy tread.

One evening, Cordt stood in Hans' room and talked to him as he had never talked to any one:

"I am your father's employer," he said, "and my father was your grandfather's. My son will never be yours. For you mean to make your own way and be your own master. You would have done that even if no one had lent you a helping hand. That is true. But then you would have become bitter, perhaps, and distrustful and narrow-minded in the use of your strength. From this I delivered you. To-day, I come to ask for a return."

Hans had taken the hand which he put out to him and stood ill at ease, without understanding. And Cordt sat down wearily and sat long without speaking further.

At last, he woke from his thoughts and looked at the young man, who could not interpret his glance, but was moved by it:

"I do not wish that you were my son," he said. "I have a son and he is a good lad and I love him. He has not your strength of character, but then he does not need it. His path was smoothed and shaded from the day when he was born and grew up. But he can give you many things which you have not."

He listened to his own words, to the way in which they kept on shaping themselves into an apology for Finn, a prayer for forbearance towards him. He suffered at this; and Hans, who saw his distress, felt, without understanding, that something important and tragic was taking place in this great house, where he and his had earned their living.

"Will you try if you can be his friend?"

Hans was quite willing.

Cordt looked at him and gauged his strength. He looked round in the little low-ceilinged room which contained nothing but what served Hans in his work. He looked out of the window, where the roofs intersected one another, dirty and grey against the sky: smoke rose from hundreds of chimneys, the noise of the courtyard and the street filled the room, the window was broken and pasted up with paper.

Then he again turned his eyes to the man who sat amidst these mean surroundings and grew up strong. And Cordt knew that he was not standing here as his benefactor and his father's employer, who was opening his rich house to him. He stood here as one who could beg and nothing more.

"You know you used to play together as children," he said.

And, when he had said that, he was overcome with emotion, because he remembered that Finn had never played. Hans thought the same thing, but could not find the words that should be spoken on this occasion and the silence became heavy and painful to both of them.

To say something at all costs, Hans asked if Finn was ill.

Then Cordt understood that Hans must long since have pronounced his judgment on the pale, silent heir of the house and that the judgment could not be good.

He rose, tired of seeking for guarded phrases. He laid his hands on Hans' shoulders and looked at him in such a way that Hans never forgot it:

"Do you be David," he said. "Come to us with your harp. And come of your own accord and come when we send for you."

CHAPTER XVIII

The first thing was that Finn had his former room arranged so that he and Hans could be there when Hans came to see him.

There was nothing said about it. For it was taken as a matter of course that no stranger should set foot in the old room. But Cordt at once thought that his hope in Hans was shattered.

Sometimes Finn was glad when Hans was there.

They could never talk together.

Hans' thoughts were constantly at work on plans and difficulties, the least of which seemed quite unsurmountable to Finn, and he had not the remotest idea as to what passed in his friend's brain. He talked to all men alike and his words were all questions or answers or opinions.

So it was Hans who spoke and, wholly taken up with himself as he was, he seldom noticed that Finn fell a-dreaming.

When Finn could get him to set to work on some calculation or other, he himself sat delighted and watched Hans while he struggled with figures and drawings.

He was amused at Hans' wrinkled forehead, his eager, impatient movements. And he waited expectantly, like one sitting on a race-ground, or wherever else men are engaged in contest, for the shout with which the engineer would fling aside the pencil when the problem was solved.

Then Finn's face beamed with delight. He was as pleased as if it had been himself that had gained the triumph and he had no notion what sort of triumph it was or what it was worth.

But sometimes, and more and more frequently, Hans was too active, too restless for him.

There were days on which Finn hid when his friend called. Often, Hans' mere presence in the room occasioned him real bodily pain. He could feel half unconscious under his powerful glance, his voice, which was so loud and jolly, his words, which all meant something.

Then he sat tortured and wretched, because it was not possible for him to ask the other to go. And it was only seldom that Hans perceived this. When it did happen, there was no end to his awkward distress; and then Finn was not content before he had succeeded in persuading him that he was quite wrong.

Then Finn submitted, in the same way in which a hopeless invalid submits to a new cure which prepares new sufferings for him and in which he does not himself believe. And, while he suffered, he thought incessantly of his father, who suffered more than he did and whom he could not help.

His best time was when they were out together.

They drove and rode; and then they were never agreed, for Finn wanted to ride slowly and drive fast and Hans wanted just the opposite. They were always eager to accommodate themselves to each other, but this came to pass only when it was Finn's wish that prevailed.

Finn did not like going out. But, once he had started, he was glad; and then he always wanted to have Hans with him. He was shy in a crowd and his friend's presence reassured him.

They generally walked in the streets, for Finn felt cold if he went outside the town. Then he took Hans' arm and kept step with him and was proud of him. He liked to hear his strong voice through the noise of the street, his quick step, the tap of his stick on the pavement.

Then Finn would sometimes begin to talk.

Mostly of his travels. And he could speak of these almost as he thought and as he spoke to his mother. It was as though the life and the noise that half drowned his words made him feel freer and safer.

And, although Hans cared but little for what Finn had seen and talked about, still there was a color and a gleam about his words that captivated him.

But, when it happened that the noise in the street was suddenly stilled, then Finn was silent and frightened. And, if, for a moment, they were separated in the crowd and Hans failed to catch a sentence and asked him to repeat it, or seized upon some phrase and asked for a further explanation and confirmation, then Finn was forthwith tired and his mood changed.

He often stopped when a piece of street-life caught his attention. He pointed it out to his friend and made it the subject of his talk. Then Hans would underline his words with some racy observation or other, which amused Finn, but afterwards annoyed him, because it spoilt the picture for him.

They never talked about women.

Finn was silent, because his thoughts were vague and modest. And Hans' experiences were not of such a nature that he cared to talk about them. Then, also, they both had an instinctive feeling that they had less in common on this subject than on any other and that they did not wish ever to cross each other's path.

On one occasion only was Finn his friend's guest in his home.

It was a regular feast in the little rooms, high up under the roof, and Finn was glad to be there.

He looked in delight at the two little old people who stood and sat with folded hands and little bows and nods and did not know how to show their respect and gratitude to the young master of the house. They took it for granted, as a settled thing, that Finn must be vexed because Hans had broken with tradition and gone his own way and they made endless covert excuses for it.

And through the excuses rang their pride in the strong son whom they handled as cautiously as though he would fall to pieces if they took firm hold of him ... their joyous dread of the greatness that awaited him.

Finn understood them and was touched by them. He sang his friend's praises and prophesied a preposterous success for him and was happy to read the gladness in the little parents' eyes.

And, while he was deep in conversation with them and amused at Hans, who was utterly confused that his friend should see the adoration of which he was the object, the picture of his own parents suddenly rose before his thoughts like great black silhouettes against the light background.

He stopped talking and then they all became silent and it was not pleasant in the room.

Afterwards, he stood with Hans and looked through the open window.

His eyes roamed over the hundreds of roofs. The sun shone on the slates and the red tiles and lit up the telephone-wires. Little garret-windows stuck out on every side ... with chintz curtains, with wall-flowers and geraniums and pelargoniums and yellow birds in white cages.

In one place there hung an elegantly-painted wooden box with ferns, which were quite brown, but stood proud and stiff, and a little fir-tree in the middle. In another, the curtain fluttered right out into the air and waved and flapped like a flag. Here, two sparrows hopped about in the gutter ... there, a caged bird was singing, shrilly and sweetly.

"How charming this is!" he said.

Hans did not exactly think so.

But, at that moment, Finn set eyes on a window a little to one side and so near that he felt as if he could reach across to it.

The window was open. There were flowers in it and there was a bird which hopped from perch to perch in its cage, silently and unceasingly. Behind the flowers sat a young girl sewing. He could see the back of her and a bit of her chin and hear the stitching of the sewing-machine:

"Look," he said, in an undertone.

Hans came up and at once looked away again:

"That's Marie," he said. "She's a seamstress."

There was nothing wrong either in the words or in the tone in which they were uttered. But he said it so loud and so carelessly that it hurt Finn. The girl opposite looked up and smiled.

Then something like a cloud passed over the whole picture, with the flowers and the bird and the sunny roofs. Finn sighed and came away from the window.

And, when they sat together at supper and had finished eating, suddenly there fell upon him an insuppressible melancholy.

He looked from one to the other and read in their faces that they were subduing their gladness on his account. He imagined what it was like when the three were alone, busy and cheerful in their work and in their faith in one another.

And behind their kind words and smiles he felt the pity for their quiet guest. But he thought of this only as pity for Cordt and of himself as one who suffered blame.

Then he hurriedly took his leave.

CHAPTER XIX

Hans and Finn were driving in the woods, when a little stray dog ran under the wheel and was badly hurt.

They both jumped out of the carriage. Hans knelt on the ground and took the gasping dog in his arms:

"Give me your pocket-handkerchief," he said.

Not receiving it at once, he looked up, impatiently.

Finn did not stir.

He stood leaning over the dog and looking into its glazed eyes with a great, deep, strange glance. He was not thinking whether it was an animal or a human being, whether it could be saved or whether he himself could do anything....

"Finn!"

He did not stir. He was staring into the great face of death. The door of the dark house was flung open and he stared and stared into the darkness. His soul was filled with a devout awe. He felt nothing, saw nothing, but life expiring before his eyes.

Hans looked at him speechlessly, terrified at the expression in his face, which he did not know how to interpret, and grew more and more agitated.

"Give me your pocket-handkerchief, Finn."

Finn started. He looked up and handed him the handkerchief:

"I didn't think of it," he said.

Hans did not reply. In a little while, the dog was dead and he flung it in among the trees in such a way that Finn could have struck him.

They got into the carriage and drove on in silence. Finn thought of nothing but what he had seen and did not suspect his friend's agitation. Then, suddenly, he told the coachman to pull up:

"You mustn't mind, Hans," he said. "I am going to get out.... I can go home by myself.... I want to be alone for a little."

Hans jumped out of the carriage and walked away without saying good-bye. Finn took no notice. He let the coachman shut the door, shrank into a corner and drove home.

Fru Adelheid came to him in the old room and could not make him speak of what lay on his mind. She smiled to him and took his hand and sang for him.

But Finn sat silent and absent.

Some time after, the friends were walking, one evening, through the streets and along the canal, where the boats lay in a row and, on the other side, an old castle stood, with broken windows and charming green roofs.

"Let us sit here for a bit," said Finn.

They sat on the quay. The water flowed black and angry beneath them. The boats rocked and bumped and swayed. Hans drummed with his cane against the embankment-wall:

"Is it like this in Venice?" he asked.

"No," said Finn. "It's finer there. Because one's strange to it."

Hans laughed gaily and Finn said nothing more and looked down into the water.

Then they suddenly heard a shout.

They both sprang up and ran and, when they had come some distance, they saw a child on the point of drowning:

"Here, Finn ... help me...."

Hans scrambled down into one of the boats and was fumbling with the oars. But Finn ran on and jumped into the water, where the child was, without a moment's reflection.

He could not swim and Hans had first to save him. Then, with the greatest difficulty, he rescued the child. They went home to Cordt's house and, when the first fright was over and it became clear that Finn had suffered no harm, they all sat in the living-room and talked about it.

Fru Adelheid held Finn's hand between her own and patted it and pressed it. Cordt walked up and down in great emotion.

"How could you take it into your head?" said Hans. "You know you can't swim."

"I never gave it a thought," said Finn, quietly.

Cordt stopped in front of his son and nodded to him. Fru Adelheid kissed him on the forehead and her eyes beamed.

Hans looked at them, crimson with anger.

He thought of how Finn might have been drowned, or the child, or both of them. Then he remembered the scene in the woods, with the dying dog. He could not understand these people's train of thought and he despised it. He looked at none of them and, with an effort, forced his voice to be calm, as he said:

"One has no right to behave like that. It is stupid."

"Yes," said Finn.

But Cordt put his hand on the engineer's shoulder and looked at him in such a way that Hans suddenly remembered his own little faint-hearted father:

"Yes," said Cordt, "it is stupid that Finn shouldn't know how to swim."

Then it was decided that Cordt's son should learn to swim.

CHAPTER XX

Fru Adelheid sat, book in hand, without reading.

It was late. Finn had been with her and had said good-night and Cordt was not at home. It was silent in the house and silent outside.

She had a feeling as though she were alone in the world.

Fru Adelheid was not happy.

The peace which the good grey years had brought had departed from the house. She could not see her way anywhere: not with Finn, not when she was alone, least of all when Cordt was in the room.

She did not feel safe even at church. It would happen to her that she left church heavier in mind than when she entered. It also happened that she simply dared not go in, but turned back, when the organ pealed to her in the porch.

She sat and stared, with her white hands folded in her lap. She wanted to try if she could think the thing out to the end. But she had tried before, with ever-decreasing success.

First, there was the going back to the old room.

This was the beginning and she could not but think that it was the whole matter, for, in truth, she had never got over it. She could not defend herself against the memories that came crowding one upon the other. Her blood grew hot, her eyes moist, without her knowing why.

She suffered from a constant terror which she could neither explain nor shake off. Now it was Finn, whose pale face frightened her. Now it was Cordt, who was silent and ever more silent and brooded over his thoughts.

Then she was overcome as by a despairing remorse and she could not see how she had offended. Then she went in a secret dread of revenge and she knew of no one who meant her any harm.

There were days on which every step she took gave a dull and threatening echo of the old days. She felt as though she were living in a house whose walls were full of secret recesses with old documents which would upset everything that existed, if they came to light ... she felt as though she were walking over mysterious vaults that concealed the traces of mysterious crimes.

Wearily, Fru Adelheid leant her head upon her hand and let her hand fall again. She half rose in her chair and hid her face in the roses that stood on the table before her. She took up the book and put it down at once.

Then Cordt came.

He nodded to her, went to the farther side of the room and sat down with a book.

She looked at him timidly. She heard him turn the pages and wondered what book it was. She asked him. He answered, without looking up, and the silence increased twofold.

Fru Adelheid sighed and rose to go to bed:

"Good-night, Cordt."

He closed the book and tossed it on the table. She stopped and looked at him. Then he asked:

"Has Hans been here to-day?"

She sat down in her chair again. He had got up and was pacing the room. She waited and listened to his footsteps.

Then she could bear it no longer:

"Cordt!"

He stopped and looked at her.

"Cordt ... Finn will die, if Hans is always with him."

"Yes," he said, softly and sorrowfully. "Finn will die and you will die and I shall die. But Hans will live."

"What are you trying to do with him, Cordt?"

"Have you forgotten what I want?"

He looked at her and his eyes hurt her.

"I wonder if your wish is also mine, Cordt," she asked.

"No."

He said that calmly, without anger, but also without hesitation.

Then she leapt up:

"Your wish was never mine ... never! You have been able to persuade me and frighten me and force me.... I never meant it, Cordt, never ... even when I agreed."

"Let the dead days be, Adelheid."

"And now ... Cordt.... Now I am farther away from you ... now you understand me less than ever ... there is something in me now that is a thousand times stronger than what parted us then."

Cordt looked at her with a tempest in his strong eyes:

"So there is in me, Adelheid."

He stood before her, drawn up to his full height. She thought he seemed taller than usual and his face looked strangely young.

"There is Finn," he said.

Fru Adelheid sat in her chair, because she could not stand.

"You speak as if he were your son and not mine," she said.

She did not take her eyes from his face. She could not get rid of the thought that he looked so young. His hair had not a sign of grey, his walk was easy and erect as in the old days, his eyes glowed with the same strength and the same confidence.

She bent forward and stared and sought. Surely she must be able to find the wounds which sorrow had given him, the marks which age had brought.

Cordt did not look at her. He stood with his hands folded about his neck and with strangely distant eyes:

"You have said it, Adelheid ... it is as you say ... there is something now that is a thousand times greater than what parted us then. We mortals always think, when misfortunes come, that no more will come now ... that it must be over now. And so there is no difference between the child with its lost doll and the man with his dead love ... none except time, which comes and goes, comes and goes, puts out a light and kindles a pyre and puts out the pyre also."

He dropped his arms and stood silent for a while:

"Adelheid...."

He said no more. He looked round the room and at her, as though he were waking from his thoughts. Then he went to the window and looked across the square, where the lights were being put out.

Fru Adelheid stared with great fixed eyes at where he stood.

She had not seen him during many years ... where had she been all those years ... what had she been doing?

Then she had seen him again, distantly and dimly at first, like the memory of a fight, a pain, on the day when she stood once more in the old room. He had come closer ... the time he warned her about Finn. And, little by little, he had approached her through Finn ... through his fears and his love, through his every word, constantly closer and more effectively.

She clutched the arms of the chair so firmly that her knuckles turned white.

Now it had come ... now the doors of the mysterious cellars grated on their rusty hinges and the crime stood revealed ... now the secret recesses in the walls were opened and the old documents bore witness to the right....

Now there was no longer anything between her and him and there was nothing outside him and her. He stood beside her ... she could reach him with her hands. She had no son and no God. His words swept over her like a storm, his eyes were bent upon her....

She wanted to get up and run away, but could not. A sort of dizziness came over her and the ground retreated under her feet.

There were voices which told her that it was surely a very old and forgotten story ... a legend preserved in the archives of the house for the entertainment and instruction of future times, which would possibly judge differently from the one who had set the legend down.

There were others, mocking and exultant voices, which whispered to her that it was all imagination and nothing else ... that Finn belonged to her and not to him, that all his confidence and all his strength would break like glass against that pale, quiet boy, who loved his mother.

There were hymns and psalms and organ-pealing and impressive words about sin and forgiveness and Christ's heavenly glory. The cool air of the church-vault passed over her burning forehead ... all the bells rang, as though for a soul in need.

She heard it all and it vanished like a sound in the air.

And all the voices were merged before her confused thoughts.

It turned into an evening in the old days ... an evening of lights and gayety. She saw the people of that time ... she heard her own voice....

Then, suddenly, it was quenched in the great silence of the old room.

The candles were burning on the mantelpiece.... She sat and stared into the red hearth. Now Cordt spoke ... Cordt in the old days:

"I will stake life and happiness to win you. I will talk to you and importune you and conquer you. I will take you in my arms and close my door to you and run after you and forgive you. And, if I do not win you, I shall cast you off."

She sprang up and clasped her head in her two hands:

"Cordt ... Cordt...."

He turned round and looked into her white face.

She raised her face to him and sought and stared after her portrait in his eyes ... only a thought from the old days ... a memory....

It was not there. For him there was nothing in the world except that which was his happiness and his fear and his struggle ... now as in the old days....

And it was no longer she.

"Adelheid ... are you ill?"

"No ... no...."

She laughed aloud. Cordt took her hands and led her to a chair. She let him do as he would and continued to look up in his face.

Then she suddenly thrust him from her.

She smiled and shook her head at her folly. She rose and walked round the room. She said she was quite well, told him to go away ... just to go away.

And Cordt went.

She stared at the door, which closed after him, as though she had seen him for the last time. Then she turned round and looked into a mirror which showed her whole figure.

Slowly she walked up to the mirror, sat down before it, with her head in her hands, and stared into her own face.

The clock struck one and two from the church-steeples and she did not hear. Then some one shouted down in the square. She rose, took a candle and left the room.

She went through the long passages and up the stairs, softly and carefully, as if she were a thief. She listened at Cordt's door and at Finn's. Then she stood outside the old room. She listened ... there was no sound. She opened the door ajar and saw that it was dark.

She went in quickly and walked straight up to the secret recess in the wall. She opened it and took the yellow document in her trembling hands.

Then she stared at Cordt's name and her own, which were written down last and struck out again.

CHAPTER XXI

Finn stood at the window in Cordt's room, with his head leaning against the frame, and looked down into the yard, where the porter's children were playing.

He had come, as usual, to say good-morning and Cordt had told him to wait while he finished a letter. The letter had been sealed for some time, but Finn had not noticed it. He was watching the game down below and bending forward to see better.

Then the children were called in. He laid his head against the window-frame again and looked up at the grey sky. He thought of Hans, who had left for Paris that morning and was to remain abroad for two years.

Cordt sat silent. From where he was, he could see Finn's profile: the forehead, which was so white, the eyelids, which lifted themselves so heavily, the mouth, which was so tired and so weak.

"Finn!"

Finn started and turned round.

"Did you see Hans off?"

"Yes."

Finn sat down by the window where he stood, with bent head and his hands upon his knees. He wound the cord of the blind round his fingers and unwound it again.

"I wonder if you will miss Hans?"

"Oh ... yes."

"I shall," said Cordt. "Hans represents the new order at its finest ... the hero in modern poetry ... the engineer, you know, whom they can never put on the stage without making him insipid ... because he never acts a part. He is strong and has the courage to employ his powers. To us he often seems lacking in refinement and he finds it difficult to grant us our due. He has no ancestors ... he is the ancestor ... he founds a dynasty."

"Yes," said Finn.

They sat silent for a while.

There was no doubt in Cordt. He knew what he wanted and wanted it. He did not seek for kind words, but strong words. Finn knew this too. He sat like a culprit awaiting sentence and was thankful for every minute that passed.

Then they looked up into each other's eyes.

They measured each other's strength. And Finn was strong in his hopelessness, even as Cordt was strong in the hope which he could not let go, because he had nothing else to fall back upon.

"Do you know that you are a born artist, Finn?"

Finn smiled sadly and shook his head.

"You are," said Cordt. "There is no doubt about it. When you were travelling abroad ... there was simply nothing in your letters but delight at the pictures you saw. Your journey was one long progress through a royal gallery. At sea, in the street, on the mountains ... everywhere you caught life and hung it on your wall and sat down to look at it."

"Did I?"

"Had you not been born with a silver spoon in your mouth, you would have been lost beyond redeeming. You would have become a painter ... no ... an author."

"Would that be so bad?"

"What use is literature to us modern people?" said Cordt. "Where does it lead us? How does it form our lives? If the old poets had lived nowadays, they would certainly have been merchants, or electricians, or arctic navigators.... Just look round you, Finn ... the books we read, the pictures we look at, the plays they perform: isn't it all like an orchestra that plays for an hour while people walk about the grounds? Tired people, who like to hear a bit of music before they go to bed. The band plays its tune and gets its pay and its applause and we are interested in seeing that the performance is well and properly given.... But ... the *poet*, Finn.... A solitary horn sounds over the hills. We drop the plough and listen and look up, because the notes seem to us so rare and so powerful and we have never heard them before and know them so well. Then our eyes glisten. And the sorrow that bent our back and the gladness that held us erect and the hope we had ... all of that suddenly acquires color and light. And we go whither the horn calls us ... over the hills ... to new green fields where it is better living."

"Father...."

Finn raised his head, but then could not find the phrase for what he wanted to say.

"Don't you think that the poet must be a *man* ... a man like the others, with courage in his breast and a sword at his thigh? Then he goes forth and sings them to battle and wedding, to dance and death. He is a part of the business, foremost in the crowd."

"The poets also sat in the ladies' chambers and sang," said Finn.

Cordt nodded:

"They did that *also*," he said. "But the poets we now have do nothing else. There will always be fiddlers as long as there are idle women and women with two husbands and wars and kings. As long as the stars wander so far through the sky and the children cannot catch the bird that flies in the bush.... But never mind that, Finn. Never mind that. Just look at those who sit in the orchestra to-day.... Would you sit among them? They are sick people singing about their sickness. One is sick with love and one with lewdness and one with drink. One chants his faith on vellum, another sells his doubts in sixpenny editions. The feeble will of the one quavers in silly verses ... the other intoxicates his pale fancy with blood and horrors drawn from the olden times. Do you think that a free man would of his own accord select his place among those artists?"

Finn looked up with his quiet eyes:

"Who is a free man, father?... Are you?"

Cordt put his hands on Finn's shoulders and bent over him and looked at him:

"You are, Finn.... You are a free man ... if you wish to be."

"Father...."

Finn put out his hands like a child asking for something. But Cordt looked at him inexorably. And so strong and radiant was his glance, that Finn tried to escape it, but could not; tried to speak, but was silent.

Then Cordt walked across the room, up and down, with great, calm strides, and spoke and was silent and never for a moment released his son from his stern grasp.

His words seized Finn and lifted him up where things were great and beautiful and bitterly cold, he thought; then let him fall again, till he relapsed into his own dark corner; and seized him anew and carried him aloft.

But, when Cordt ceased, it was to Finn as though he heard a flourish of trumpets from the clouds proclaiming that other words were now coming, greater still and austerer, more loving, ever heavier to bear.

"You are right, Finn.... I am not a free man, I never was. I am bound up in the tradition that built my house and bore my race and, when I could not support the tradition, things broke for me. But that did not make me free.... Those were heavy days, Finn. I could not understand it, you see, and I fought to the end. I was young and strong and I was in love. You are fond of the old room ... you can hear the legends up there singing their powerful, melancholy song.... Remember, Finn, I am one of those on whom the legend is laid. I have lived in the secrecy of the old room.... I have stood, in my calm, proud right ... up there, where the room stood, unseen by any one except the master of the house and his wife ... always remote and locked and hidden in its time-honored might ... always open to him who owned it.... I left it like a beaten man. But I could not retire into a corner and mourn, for I had you, Finn. You were only a little child then, so I could not know how your paths would go. I knew only one thing, that you would never sit with your wife up there, where people became so small when they sat down in the big chairs and where it was so pleasant and so safe. I was the last. With me, the tradition of the old room was finished.... Then I had to try if I could find my way in the world which I did not understand. I had to go through all that which I disliked so desperately and which had killed my happiness. For myself, I had nothing to gain: I was a bound man and a wounded. But I had you, Finn.... And I had to know if they were building properly and honestly somewhere behind all the dancing and flirting and singing which I saw before my eyes. Or if it was no different from what my eyes saw and if I should not be doing best to carry my child out into the mountains and let the wild beasts tear it to pieces.... I was alone in this. Your mother went to live in an old house beside the old house where her happiness could not grow. There she found peace. But I needed no refuge. Where I was, I was at home: I only wanted to see the place where you and your children should flourish.... I did not spare myself, Finn. I sought honestly, south and north, east and west. I took their books ... the light ones burst like soap-bubbles in my hands and the powerful ones my thoughts had to struggle to understand. Not one of their green visions but has been with me in my room, not one of their bright swords but has flashed before my eyes.... I did not allow myself to be blinded by my own bitterness, or tricked by catch-words, or frightened by abuse. I went on as long as I could see the way ... and longer, Finn. I peered out into the farthest, where those who thought as I did saw nothing but horror and insanity.... And Finn ... I don't know.... Perhaps it was your mother's God that helped me ... perhaps it was my ancestor, who himself had sailed into harbor and raised our house on new ground for many a good, long day. Perhaps it was your little hand, which lay so trustingly in mine, when you used to come to me in those anxious, lonely days and say good-morning and good-night.... I don't know. I daresay it was my love for you that lifted me above myself. I climbed as high up the mountains as a mortal can climb. It all lay under my feet like a cloud ... longing and happiness and daily bread and daily trouble. I could not see the valley in which my house was built. But out of the cloud, over the mountain, I saw the road where we hustle and strive, generation after generation, ever forward towards the goal which we cannot see, but which is there, because the road is there.... And I saw land ... the promised land of you and your children ... from the mountain where I stood. A land I did not know ... a land strange to my eyes ... people with other habits and other beliefs, with a different form of love and a different code of honor.... I saw it through the storm that flung the door of the old room wide open.... That was a strange time, Finn ... the strongest in my life and the happiest."

Cordt stood at the window with his arms crossed over his chest. He looked at his son and smiled sadly. Finn sat still, with his head thrown back in his chair and his eyes closed.

"Then I equipped you for the journey, Finn.... I did not show you this way or that, for I was a bound man and could not go with you. I gave you books and masters, who opened all the gates of the world to you. I let you look into the mist where you wanted to ride. I feared nothing, because I wanted nothing for myself and because I had seen through the mist.... You grew up and I saw that you grew good and clever. Then I sat down and waited and longed for the day when I should wave to you from the balcony of my old house, when you marched forth to conquer your new land.... I was right to wait for the day.... Ah.... I have seen them, the poor devils, hungry and wounded, rush blindfold towards the new, which they did not know, because it could not possibly be worse than the old. I have heard them call for new laws because they had violated the old ... they were driven from their huts and sat on the deck of the emigrant-ship with their bundle and their uncertain hope for a better fate in the new world.... But you.... You had done no wrong and had nothing to revenge. Free as a king's son, you rode over the bridge with your retinue and rode through the world and planted your banner wherever you chose to dwell. Born of your mother's longing for excitement ... in your father's house, whose walls are as thick as the walls of a castle ... with the strong air of the old room in your lungs and without its yoke upon your neck ... a rich and spotless nobleman, taking his place of his own free will in the ranks of the revolution."

He was silent. His steps sounded heavily through the stillness:

"Are you with me, Finn?"

"Yes, father."

"Come."

Finn rose. Cordt put his arm over his shoulder and they paced the room together.

"I had so many dreams, Finn. And I gained such confidence, because my own happiness was shattered and I had you. I had become an old man, but my mind was not blunted. I had suffered shipwreck, but I was not afraid of the sea. I believed in life ... in God, if you like."

They did not walk well together and Cordt removed his arm. Finn sat down in his chair again and listened. Cordt went on walking:

"Then came the days which you know ... the days of the present.... You grew up into the quiet man you are. Your eyes looked heavily upon life, you shrank back timidly when you saw that there was fire and smoke on earth.... You kept your scutcheon untarnished, but that is easily done, when one doesn't fight. You were never in places where one does not wish to be seen ... that is true. But you never went outside your door, Finn ... never. There was no fire in your blood, no desire in your thoughts. You were tired, Finn ... merely tired.... I grew frightened for you.... As the years passed, you had become more to me than a son. You were not only flesh of my flesh and bone of my bone ... you were a link in the human chain that goes on through the ages, ever onward. Your hand was in mine, but your life was more precious than mine. For you had to carry a greater burden and to carry it into new ways.... Remember, Finn, I had been on the mountain and seen through the mist. It was more than the question of an inheritance, more than family pride and family loyalty. You and I were allied in a great cause. And I sat with the map before me and followed the course of the battle ... like an old soldier, who can no longer sally forth himself, but who has his son and his colors and his emperor under fire.... Remember how I had arrived at where I was. Remember what I had lost, what I had let go, how completely I had sacrificed myself for you. I had you, Finn ... had I anything else?... When I, then, became frightened for you, I plunged into my wonderful treasure and endowed you lavishly. I told you the legend of the old house and thought it would call you to arms, like the blast of the bugle over the camp. I revealed your father's and your mother's fate to you, that you might see how people fight for happiness. I sent you out into the world, where life is bigger and stronger than at home, so that life might make you into a man.... But never ... never did I put any constraint upon you. Never did I usurp the place of Providence.... And you turned over the pages of the picture-book and came home paler than before and wearier. The old room was merely a charming poem to you, that sang you into deeper dreams. Up there ... where the strong men of our race met their wives, when the sun went down upon the business of the day, and talked gladly and earnestly when their hearts impelled them to ... there you sit, alone, all day long, with your slack hands."

Then he laid his hands firmly on Finn's shoulders. And Finn looked up with moist eyes and quivering mouth.

"To-day, Finn, I have given you your inheritance. From to-day, I look upon you as of age. You were such that one could not use coercion with you ... and, in fact, there was none that wanted to use it. Nor could one be angry with you ... you were the same ... it was the same ... always. To-day, that is past. Go out and buy yourself a house and take a wife and have children by her. And remember that, if there were some in the family that fell, there was none that flinched."

"Father.... I understand you ... but I cannot do what you want."

Cordt took a step back and tossed his thick hair from his forehead:

"You pale people *understand* everything, because no faith blinds your eyes: you are so kind and clever, you think. You judge leniently, you do not judge at all, you know that the truth is nowhere and everywhere. You justify every silly thought you have entertained ... you sit for all time and contemplate your navel ... and then you let the murderer go and the thief escape. God help you poor wretches! The stupidest, the most ignorant dervish is cleverer and kinder than you!"

Finn wanted to say something, but Cordt made a preventive gesture with his hand:

"A man *must* not understand everything. He must choose and judge and reject. If he doesn't do that, there is no happiness in the world and no loyalty and no peace. And, if he cannot hate, he cannot love either."

He went to the window and looked out. And, as he stood there, Finn came up to him and seized his hand and looked at him pleadingly:

"I can't do what you want," he said.

But Cordt withdrew his hand and moved away from him:

"You have no right to say that to me, Finn. I won't listen to it. For what I want is only that you should live. Take the inheritance which I have given you and use it as you can. One day, you shall be called upon to answer for your son, as I to-day for you."

Finn smiled sadly:

"I shall never have a son," he said, softly.

Cordt did not hear what he said. He was struggling with a memory ... passed his hand over his face and stared before him. He saw Fru Adelheid ... that evening in the old room, when she had said what Finn was saying now ... the same hopeless, impotent words: "I cannot do what you want."

He sat down and fell back in his chair.

All the despair of the old days came over him like a tremendous weariness. He was struggling against what was stronger than himself. He had nothing to set against that eternal, hopeless, "I cannot do what you want."

Then he sprang up and stood in front of Finn with blazing eyes:

"If it's your mother who paralyzes your will, then fly from her, hate her, thrust her from you...."

"Father ... father...."

"Hate her, I say. She was smitten with the pestilence from her youth. She understood everything ... like you. To her nothing was small or great, nothing near or far. Her will was gone, like yours. She knew where the glory lay, if she could reach it, but she could not. She hearkened to the times and the times made her their own. She was always sick ... sick unto death."

He crossed the room and said nothing more.

They were both of them very pale and both longed to be alone. They had nothing more to say to each other.

And Finn was not angry on his mother's account. He thought only of the one thing, that he could not do what Cordt wanted and could not appease his sorrow ... could not even tell him that he loved him. And then he longed to sit still ... in the old room ... with his mother, who was so pretty and whom he had never offended:

"Are you angry with me, father?"

Cordt looked at him long and intently. Then he said:

"Yes."

But, when Finn was gone, he sat with his face buried in his hands and wept.

CHAPTER XXII

Cordt entered, dressed to go out, and hurriedly crossed the room.

Fru Adelheid sat writing. She looked up, as he came in, and went on writing.

"Where is Finn?"

"Upstairs, I suppose ... in his room," she answered, without looking at him.

He stood at the window for a moment. Then he flung himself into a chair and got up again and stood by the table at which she was sitting:

"Have you been with him to-day?"

"No."

She closed her blotting-book and turned her chair so that her face was in shadow. Then she said:

"Finn is too much alone."

"Yes."

He nodded and said yes again; then stood with his head bowed deep in thought.

"It is so quiet here," said Fru Adelheid. "You are not happy and Finn notices it. And Hans is away...."

"Yes ... yes...."

She crossed her arms over her breast and sat silent and looked at the tip of her foot.

"Adelheid...."

Cordt drew himself erect:

"We will fill the house with gayety," he said. "We will go and pay visits to-morrow morning ... you and Finn and I ... to old friends and new. We will have young and cheerful people here and pretty women and clever men ... lights and music."

She looked up at him. He smiled and put his hand on her shoulder.

"Yes," she said.

Cordt talked about it a little and then went out hurriedly.

Fru Adelheid remained sitting long. The room grew dark. The lamps before the gateway were lit and their flickering gleams danced on the ceiling. The fire in the hearth smouldered under the ashes. Where she sat, no light fell; her white dress shone faintly through the gloom.

She thought of Cordt's smile ... he had said that to her much as though he were asking one of the people in the office to take pains in a difficult matter.

She thought of Finn, who looked at her with such strange eyes, as though the relations between him and his mother had changed and he could not understand it.

She thought of herself. She felt like a tree in autumn, when the leaves fall ... a tree that had always thought itself green and beautiful until now, when it saw its glory flutter before the wind.

And, day after day and every hour of the day, she rebuilt it all as it might have been.

She built up the temple of the old room again and locked the door with seven seals. She put time back and sat with her little boy in her lap and resented old Marie's undressing him and singing him to sleep. She put time forward and celebrated the day when Finn should lead his wife into the secret chamber of the house and tell her all about it, in all its beauty and solemnity, and write his name and hers on the yellow document.

Fru Adelheid smiled sadly.

She thought she was like the man who had put the celestial globe up there in the old room ... the man whose intellect was obscured and who sat and played with the stars until he died.

But her thoughts always went the same way, while the darkness fell ever closer about Cordt's house.

She wondered, would it be any use now, if the house were filled with lights and gayety? Or would the darkness lurk in every gloomy corner and spring forth when the feast was over and for ever hide the three who moved about the house, each his own way, anxiously and alone?

She did not know. But she always thought of it. And there was nothing tempestuous in her hope and in her fear and in her regret.

Fru Adelheid was calm now, always.

CHAPTER XXIII

Then the stately house on the square was lit up with gayety.

The horses trampled in the gateway and the servants ran up and down the carpeted stairs. The great drawing-rooms streamed with lights and flowers and music and the floor was filled with dancers.

It was a wealth and splendor even greater than in the old days, for now the master of the house was a more lavish host than he had ever been before. He could never have things fine enough, luxurious enough. He saw to everything, was everywhere and moved among his guests so that they could see that he delighted in them.

The entertainments at Cordt's house became legendary. And all that were rich and beautiful and noble and intelligent came when he invited them and came gratefully and were glad to stay.

The men gathered close about the lady of the house, who was charming in her white gown, with her white hair.

Those who had paid her their homage in the old days raised their grey heads when she passed them and followed her tall figure with a gleam of their youthful fire in their eyes. And those who were now young wondered when they heard the old ones tell that she was once a thousand times prettier.

Or not prettier, perhaps. But such that every man on whom her eyes fell was, from that moment, hers and that every glance she vouchsafed was remembered for all time.

Now she was more remote in her smiles. Her glance was deeper, but it was as though it did not see. Her red mouth no longer promised happiness as it used to. Any one would think it a happiness to win her. But no one would believe it possible.

And, while they saw her thus in the light of their youth, they wondered what could have happened in the years that had passed and why the house had so long been closed and why it had now so suddenly opened its doors wide to the world which holds revel daily.

But their thoughts never grew to the shadow of a slander.

They asked her to sing. And, as she sat at the piano and looked through the room with her great, strange eyes, the old friends of the house remembered the glowing songs of her youth, which had set their blood aflame as she exulted and wept in them with desire and love.

But now, when she sang, the young ones listened, enraptured with her voice, which was so bright and so clear and so wonderfully still:

The wildest water on earth to-day
(God grant me His grace consoling!)
Flows deep and dreary through gorges grey,
But whither and whence they alone can say
Who first set its wild waves rolling.

For no ship ever its tideway knew,
Its marge bore never a blossom.
And never a bird from the beaches flew,
And never a mirrored star it drew
From Heav'n to its own black bosom.

It wells from eyes that are glazed with pain
(God shield me in all disaster!)
When a man has rent like a rag in twain
His own life's bliss, by his own hand slain,
Being never his fortune's master.

There was a brief silence when she ceased. Then they crowded round her in admiration and with endless requests for more.

Fru Adelheid rose. She talked and smiled and thanked them. But her glance wandered far beyond all these people, who meant nothing to her, to Cordt, who stood at the far end of the room and was talking to some one and did not see her and had not heard her.

But Finn had heard her. And Finn had seen her great, humble, plaintive look.

He did not take his eyes off her and strange thoughts hurried through his head. He now understood what had happened in this house. He knew why Fru Adelheid had come to him so seldom, lately, in the old room. Why she had sat so silent, steeped in distant thoughts ... why her glance had been so uncertain and so timid, her words so wavering, her hand so slack in his.

And he felt that the last bond was broken that bound him to mankind.

He had lost his mother, now that he was pushing hardest towards her. When she came to him now, it was Cordt she looked for. Were he to go to her now and lie down before her with his cheek on her hand, as he had so often done, she would lift him up and bid him go out into the world and live.

He had a feeling as though he had been betrayed, but, at the same time, he wept with her in his heart. He looked at his father and thought how much more of a man he was than she suspected in her poor, tardy repentance. He looked at his mother and felt a curious loving contempt for her ... such as men feel for a woman who comes to them and begs for something a thousand times less important than what she once possessed and despised.

Then he had to go into the crowd of people, who offered him their smiles and asked for his.

And so strong was the feeling of loneliness in him that he mingled readily with the guests of the house and was more cheerful than usual and more talkative.

He was as pleased to move about these bright rooms as elsewhere, because he was no longer at home anywhere. He might just as well exchange a few words with these smartly-dressed ladies and gentlemen, since he had to talk and since he could no longer tell any one what was passing within him and since no one could tell him what he wanted to hear.

The women crowded round him as the men did round Fru Adelheid. They wound a circle of white arms and bright eyes round the young heir of the house, who was so pale and so handsome and such that women longed for that which he did not show. They met him with charming, flattering words and smiled upon him and he did not hear the words and broke through the circle without a trouble and without a sigh.

The men offered him their friendship and he shook their hands and talked to them and went away and forgot their faces. Cordt found him in every corner, where he had hidden for a moment without intending to or thinking about it, and carried him smilingly and teasingly and jestingly into the throng. And he smiled to his father and went with him and remained always alone.

He saw himself and only himself. He seized upon every thought that arose in him and discussed it as if it had been thought by another. He contemplated every mood that welled up in his soul as if he had read it in a book.

He climbed high up the peaks upon which men cannot live ... the peaks whence they topple down one day or where they perish in the bright frost. For there is no sound up there and no air, no day and no paths. Only light and always light.

But, when it happened that Cordt's glance fell upon him, without his knowing it, the loneliness was suddenly extinguished in his soul.

Then he knew who he was and where he was and the pain of life gnawed into his soul. For he constantly read the eternal, hopeless, fond question in his father's eyes. He realized what he had forgotten, that the house was making holiday for his sake and his sake alone. Every strain that sounded, every rose that blushed, every pretty woman who moved across the floor: they were all his father's servants, who came to him with message after message that life's banquet was served if he would but take his seat at the board and drain its golden cup.

Then he thought sadly of his tranquil, beautiful mother, who had gone from him, out into life, which did not touch him. How good it would have been if they could sit together now and talk and be silent, while the fountain rippled in the square and the queer things in the old room whispered their strange and mighty legend!

It would have been good for him. And good for her, he thought. And best of all, perhaps, for Cordt, who did not see her.

His thoughts gathered in love for Cordt, who was struggling to the death in his hopeless fight. He felt as though his father were a hero in the wars and wished that he were his meanest page to buckle on his armor for him and bathe his wounds and sit beside him with his lute, when he would sleep.

But the rout ran its course and it was late before the gate closed behind the last carriage.

It fell heavily and harshly as though it were striking angrily at the guests' heels. It grated its hinges long and shook its bolts as though it thought of never opening again, but of shutting out the world for ever from that old house, in which no light could drive away the increasing gloom, no joyous trumpets drown the hoarse voices that threatened in the corners.

Then they sat together for a while longer, they three who dwelt in the house, and talked with empty words and empty eyes.

Fru Adelheid it was who first ceased, because her thoughts were the strongest. And Finn it was who said the most ... as though to expiate the fault that oppressed him.

But it was Cordt who was bitterest in his care, while indifferent words passed between those who stood as close together as it was possible for mortals to stand and who feared the silence and who had nothing more to say to each other.

Then Cordt said good-night and Finn. But Fru Adelheid told the servants to leave her for a little and the candles burnt where the rout had been.

Restlessly she wandered about the room and again thought of the days that were gone and could never return. And she readily surrendered herself to her fancies, for there was in her now but one hope and one faith and one repentance.

She fancied that one of the long evenings was over in which gay acquaintances filled her rich house and Cordt and she exchanged glances which only they understood.

She had been to the nursery and leant over her little boy, who was sleeping with red cheeks. Now she would take the reddest flower there was and then go up the secret stair ... up to where the old room stood, in its wonderful glory.

There he sat and waited for her.

She saw him as she entered ... he raised his face to her and nodded and then lapsed again into his heavy thoughts. And she stood silent at the window, where the red flowers blushed before her feet and the square lay below her in the darkness of the night and the fountain sang its refrain, which never begins and never stops.

Then she rose and crossed the room. She heard his voice when he talked to her, as he so often talked ... ever the same judgment upon the dance that passed over the world, the same mighty song in praise of great marriage, the same passionate, loving prayer that she would only see it while there was yet time and let those dance who had nothing better to do and take the proud place which he offered her by his side ... in the old chair, in which people became so small and so strong, because they sat with their feet on an altar that was raised in faith and built up of faith and fenced in with faith throughout the changing times.

Then, when he had said that and sat by the chimney, where the fire glowed and the candles shed their rays sparingly in the corners of the old room ... she would stand for a little at the window, while all was silent in the room, and look at him, who was the man in her life and had never ceased to be so. And then she would go up to him ... slowly and quietly, because she honored the ground she trod on ... kneel down where he sat and raise to him the eyes whose beauty he had loved, whose glance he had sought in such great hope and such great fear.

Then she would tell him exactly how it was ... how strong it was and how silent:

"Cordt ... you strong, you irresistible man ... I love you as you would be loved. I thank you, because you talked to me and never grew weary. Because you always besought me. Because you waited for me and trusted that the day would come when the silence of the old room should turn to gladsome song in my soul and all the other sounds in the world like a distant buzz in the woods. Now I am here ... Cordt ... you strong, you irresistible man. Now I am yours, as I was before, and I am yours in the old room. There is nothing threatening or gloomy now in the strange things up here from the vanished days. I can sing to the old spinet so that no strings snap and no memories are mortally startled, for I sing only of you and of my boy and of my happiness. I can cherish the thread upon great-grandmother's spinning-wheel because I have woven the cloth of happiness in my own room. I can lovingly hide the wax doll in the folds of the curtain, because I have lived to see the day when I went gladly and readily to the secret chamber of the house and sat there long and was contented.... But the jar with the naked man writhing through thorns: I set that up here when I was not yet what I am. It shall stand here in memory of the evil time that pulled at Fru Adelheid's soul and lured her desires with sounds from the square outside.... And our little boy, who sleeps with red cheeks, shall grow to man's estate and come up here one day, when you and I are dead, and sit with his wife in the chairs in which we sat. Then he shall know that his mother was tempted, it is true, but not destroyed."

Fru Adelheid sat in her corner and dreamt in the silent, empty rooms.

Her white gown spread over the floor about her feet. Her eyes shone.

But high up, on the balcony of the old room, stood Finn and stared into the night that stretched round about him like a waveless sea.

It was silent. He did not think, did not dream. His soul mingled with the darkness, which was not evil and not good ... only silent.

He was like a dead man who had been put on guard on the brink of the tower and who still stood there, staring with glazed eyes. The fountain rippled ... it was as though the water rose over the edge of the basin and would rise and rise until it reached the dead man up there and washed him away.

Then a man came across the square.

He walked and sang, until he set eyes upon the man who stood up there, high and dark and motionless. Then he stopped and looked at him and shouted something.

And the man on the balcony answered with a shout. And the man below was seized with fear and ran away and vanished in the darkness.

CHAPTER XXIV

Cordt looked into the room where Fru Adelheid sat:

"Where is Finn?"

"I think he's in the old room."

Cordt closed the door and walked quickly down the passage. She was sitting by the window and saw him in the square below, where he stood and looked up at the house. Then he walked away, in such a manner that she could see that he had no object for his walk.

The servant came and lit the candles. Fru Adelheid sat down by the fireplace with her hands in her lap and listened for a sound in the quiet house.

Soon after, Cordt came home.

She heard his voice in the passage. Then he went into his own room ... now he was outside again. She understood that he was on his way to Finn; but the next moment he came in to where she was sitting and sat down at a distance from her:

"Have you been up to him to-day, Adelheid?"

"No."

Cordt moved restlessly in his chair, rose to go and sat down again. Fru Adelheid struggled with herself not to go over to him and take his hand and talk to him. Then he said:

"He has been so odd, lately. Brighter than usual, but more absent, nevertheless. He is not shamming, but still he is not himself."

Cordt went on talking about it, without looking at her and not so much in order to tell it to her as because he could not keep silent. She saw this exactly and turned away her face and cried quietly. Then he asked:

"Haven't you noticed it?"

"I think he is much as usual."

Cordt rose and crossed the room. He stood for a time by the chimney, where she sat, and stared into the fire. She looked up at him with bright, moist eyes. Then he went over and sat where he had been sitting before and it was silent in the room.

"I wonder, oughtn't you to go up to him, Adelheid?"

He could not hear her reply and looked across at her. She had stood up and was coming towards him. He saw that she was very pale and that she was crying, but did not think about it and forgot it again at once.

Then she sat by him ... so close that her white gown lay over his feet. She crossed her hands in her lap and parted them again and did not look at him while she spoke:

"Cordt...." she said.

And, when she had said that, she began to tremble and pressed her hands together.

"Yes?"

"*You* ought to go up to him, Cordt."

He was silent for a moment. Then he bent closer to her and lowered his voice, as though there were some one in the room who could hear what he was saying and must not:

"I dare not. I have frightened him. He starts when he sees me ... he stands outside my door and collects his courage when he comes to me to say good-morning. I will go quite away from him for a little while ... go for a journey, I think, until he becomes more tranquil."

She looked at him and pictured him roaming round the world so that Finn might recover his tranquillity. She saw him strolling in distant towns, where life flowed on around him, alone, knowing no peace, ever thinking of his son ... longing for the day when he could come home, dreading how he would find him then.

Fru Adelheid slipped from her chair and lay on the floor before him, with her cheek against his hand and her eyes streaming with tears.

Cordt did not see. He stared into the room across her head, with the strained, racked look which he now always wore when he was alone:

"He does not like our parties, Adelheid," he said, meditatively. "We only did him harm."

"Yes."

"But, if you would go up to him, Adelheid ... very quietly ... and sit with him a little, so that he could not give way to his thoughts. Or help him, so that his thoughts could find utterance. You two always got on well together, you know, and he was glad to see you whenever you came."

"He is no longer glad to see me, Cordt."

He looked at her in surprise and encountered her moist glance.

"If I went up now, Cordt ... I could not sit with Finn as I used to. For I am no longer the same."

"Ah, well!" was all he said.

He spoke calmly and indifferently, as though he had had no particular faith in his remedy and must look round for something else.

"Cordt!..."

It was a scream.

He started. And, as if he had now first seen that she was kneeling before him, he pushed back his chair and rose to his feet.

He crossed the room and then came back and stood and looked at her with a sense of dislike that increased every minute. She crept to the chair from which he had risen and laid her head on it. She closed her eyes before his glance and wept silently and without stopping.

"You...?" he said slowly.

She received the blow which the word gave her without breathing a sound. Once she opened her eyes and immediately closed them again. Pale and still she lay before his feet.

Then his eyes blazed with anger and scorn:

"What a number of years have passed since we two first met, Fru Adelheid ... what a number of miserable years!"

"Yes," she said and raised her head for a moment and laid it on the chair again.

"You went away ... in search of your red happiness. You were not content with your husband, whom you loved and who loved you ... you must have all men on their knees before your beauty ... you must needs see the desire in their eyes and their unchaste hands cramped because they dared not lay them upon Cordt's wife."

"Yes," she said.

"Well, did you find the lover who bound your will to his foot? And did he spurn you when he had seen to the depths of your charming eyes? Or did you leave him of your own accord ... and go farther out into the world ... in search of that which was greater still and redder?"

"I had no lover," she said, in a low voice.

He tossed back the hair from his forehead and clenched his fists:

"No," he said. "You did not. That is your disgrace and your judgment."

"Cordt ... Cordt ... suppose I had had...."

"Yes ... if you had had a lover and were here to-day, then I should take your hand and lead you to our son and say to him, 'Here is your mother, who has been unhappy. She loved your father and her love died when the man came who was more to her than he. She has not known a really happy day in all these years, because her fate was too strong for her. Now she has come to ask for your affection and needs it.'"

He crossed the room and then came and stood by her again:

"Get up, Adelheid."

She rose from the floor and sat down in her chair again, with her white hands crossed in her lap, silently and quietly. He looked at her and it was as though her humble obedience added to his anger:

"Where did you go on the day when you broke the bonds of your marriage, because the air in the old room was too pure for you and too strong? Where have you been since?"

"I went to God."

Cordt laughed:

"Show me your God."

He bent over and looked her in the face:

"I don't believe in your God," he said.

She did not take her eyes from his and stretched out her trembling hands to him and her red mouth quivered with weeping:

"Then I don't believe in Him either, Cordt."

He turned away from her. Quietly she bowed her head, her tears fell upon her hands, she listened and moaned under the blows which she had received and longed for more.

But Cordt sat at the window and looked out where the rain came pouring down and the flame of the lamps flickered in the wind. His anger was over. He could not remember what they had been talking of. His thoughts were where they always were and all the rest was nothing.

Then he suddenly stood by her again and struck his hand on his temples and looked at her with fear in his eyes:

"Adelheid ... do you think Finn won't come to us at all to-night?"

She understood that it was too late ... irremediably, hopelessly too late. She would never be able to tell him what was burning in her soul. He would never know that she did not come, because she was weary and because she was afraid, but that she had honestly wiped out the bad years of her life and stood again as he would have had her the time ... the time he wanted to have her thus.

"He will come and say good-night," she said calmly.

Fru Adelheid raised her folded hands to her mouth.

Things could not remain thus for ever. But she could wait. She could go barefoot over the stones, if only once she reached a place in his house where she could stay. There must be a road somewhere that led to him.

And the evening sped on.

She sat beside him again and held his hand in hers, happy that he allowed her to keep it. She wanted to push his hair off his forehead, where the wrinkles lay so sharply marked, but did not. She wanted to put her hands on his tired eyes, but dared not.

They talked of Finn and she talked softly and soothingly to him as to a child, happy to be going the way he wanted. She found such gentle words and such impressive ones ... she found her smile again and looked at him and met his smile, which came stealing to his face like a sun-gleam and vanished again at once.

He heard but little of what she said. But the sound of her voice did him good. He heard it and the rain, which beat against the panes, and it grew warm and peaceful around him.

His fears, which had aroused and spied and driven his every thought and turned and weighed his every doubt, slumbered in this quiet hour. He sat there like an old man who has suffered so much that his faculties have been blunted to pain and who takes his solace as it comes and is thankful.

He looked at her as he used to look at his mother when he was young and unhappy. He thought of her as of a young girl who knew the old man so little and owed him nothing, but went to his chair and laid her roses in his hand, so that things might be a little pleasanter for him.

And once he moved uneasily in his chair and looked at her quite differently and said:

"Adelheid ... why have I no child but him?"

He said that very quietly and, a little after, he said it again. He said it to himself and not to her. She saw this and wept, because she knew he did not perceive it.

And the evening sped on.

They sat quietly and she was silent and talked again of their son up there in the old room. Then she said:

"Cordt, let us go up to him!"

"Both of us?"

She listened anxiously whether he would say any more ... whether he would reflect who she was and thrust her from him in anger, as he had done before.

But he sat silent and looked at the red glow in the fireplace.

Then she rose and put out her hands to him:

"Come ... Cordt ... let us go. We will sit with him a little and talk to him, quietly and cheerfully, till the shadows disappear. Then we will come down here again and they will return, when he is alone. But we will go up every day and fight with them for him and win him."

He rose heavily and took her hand.

Fru Adelheid led him through the room like a child. They went through the long passage and up the secret stairs.... She was always a little in front of him. Her eyes shone with happiness. The bells rang out in her soul and she held Cordt's hand so fast as though she would never let it go.

They came to the door of the old room and knocked and listened. She looked at him and bent over his hand and kissed it with streaming tears.

Then she opened the door briskly and went in with head uplifted and drew him after her.

Over by the window sat Cordt's son, in one of the big chairs. He had shot himself.